SAVAGE COAST

A Ryan Savage Thriller

JACK HARDIN

AUTHOR'S NOTE

For those of you anxiously awaiting the next Ellie O'Conner installment—those of you missing Ellie, Tyler, Fu and Gloria, Citrus, and Major—you don't have long to wait. The title for the 7th Ellie book is *Dark Horizon* and will be out soon.

You'll find the Ryan Savage series a little punchier than the Ellie series: quicker reads, more action, all standalone installments. I hope you enjoy your time in Ryan Savage's world. He's a pretty cool dude, if I do say so myself.

-Jack

CHAPTER ONE

THE SCREAM SENT an icy chill tracking down my spine, like an ice cube melting on the back of my neck.

She was going to die, and there was nothing I could do about it.

At least, not with my hands tied behind my back and my ankles tethered to the chair legs. They had even wrapped half my face in duct tape, which left me sucking air through the only useful nostril I had left; the other one was stuffed with rapidly congealing blood. Think of snorkeling with a clogged straw as your only breathing apparatus and you'll get the idea.

I heard her scream out from the other room again. This one was different from the ones that had come before. Those had been cries of fear and anger. This one was pure terror now, most assuredly a last-ditch effort to ward off some depraved and imminent action on the part of her kidnappers.

My crazed eyes looked to the other side of the room, and as they fell on my best friend, they burned with an even hotter fury. His dead body was sprawled out across the dirty stone floor, two bullet holes leaking blood from his chest. I had been forced to watch as they shot him just two minutes before, helpless to do anything about it.

The scene caused my wrists to work even more furiously against the ropes that were binding them together. But whoever had knotted them knew exactly what they were doing. I wasn't getting out of this.

Another scream from the room behind me, and I heard the tear of clothing as she fought her assailants with everything she had left.

My bloodied chin fell to my chest as I felt the fight finally start to seep out of me.

I had failed everyone who trusted me.

If only she hadn't found that damn notebook...

CHAPTER TWO

Five Days Earlier

THERE's nothing like the sound of a bullet whizzing by your face to remind you of your own mortality.

Beads of sweat gathered on my forehead as I peered around the palm tree, raised my M27, and sighted a shooter in an upstairs window. I pulled the trigger and watched my target take the round in the neck, spin, and tumble out the window to the cobbled drive below.

All around me gunfire was chattering, tearing up the trunks of palm trees, perfectly manicured grass, and pinging off the Bentley that was parked at the top of the circular drive near the front door. Ducking, I scurried behind one of the armored vans my team had come in on and checked my load, cursing under my breath as I plucked a fresh magazine off my chest rig and swapped it out.

The M27 is a lightweight Infantry Automatic Rifle, chambered for 5.56×45mm NATO and fitted with an ACOG

Squad Day Optic and a reflex sight on top for close-quarters engagement. It is the assault rifle currently favored by the Marines. Compared to previous variants like the HK416 and M4, the weapon is lightweight and has a fair edge on reliability. I'm not a Marine, but still, I absolutely love it.

With a fresh magazine inserted, I pulled back the charging handle and took a few moments to catch my breath as I decided on my next course of action.

The raid on Rico Gallardo's beachside mansion was supposed to be in and out. Grab and go. I was sent down here to Guatemala two weeks ago to assist the U.S. Secret Service in planning the raid on the counterfeiter's opulent home.

Gallardo was single-handedly responsible for flooding the U.S. market with billions of counterfeit bills each year. He was one of the most powerful men in the small Central American country, and his reputation for violence was matched only by the most ruthless of the Mexican drug lords. He paid his people well, lubricating violent and evil orders with fat paychecks.

But his little money spigot was about to get turned off.

Our initial intent was to grab Gallardo without requesting help from or notifying the local authorities, but the order had come down from Washington to work hand-in-hand with the *Policía Nacional Civil*—Guatemala's national police force. That immediately made the risks go up a hundredfold. You bring in the local police and you're bound to have a squeaky rat somewhere in the mix who's on the very payroll you're trying to shut down. It seemed that no one down here was immune from the rampant corruption found among police units and politicians. Everyone has their price, and down here, that price was usually to be found at dollar-store prices. Another bullet pinging off my cover was reminder enough that someone in the *Policía Nacional Civil* had chosen fidelity to Gallardo over the people in his country he had taken an oath to help keep safe.

No one had expected the crime boss to just throw up his hands and let us take him without a fight, but we had also planned to catch him off guard so we didn't end up in a full-out war like we were in now.

A flurry of hasty orders charged the air around me, and men repositioned themselves as they tried new ways to infiltrate the mansion. Across the lawn, a Secret Service agent fell to a fresh wave of bullets, and my blood heated with anger. I saw movement in my periphery and shifted to my right as Secret Service Special Agent Bud Cole slid in beside me and took a moment to catch his breath. He was a hefty bald man. A fantastic agent, but he'd spent a little too much time behind a desk the last couple of years. "Savage," he said, grinning, "what are you doing in the dugout? You're supposed to be on the field."

"Too many players out there," I replied. "We've got to find a way into that house or we're going to be sitting ducks out here. Tell the snipers to focus everything they have on the second floor. We're not getting enough cover fire."

Cole leaned into his shoulder mic and barked off a couple of orders then checked the load on his own rifle. I looked over at him. "I'm not leaving here until I've got Gallardo's head to mount on my wall. You hear me?"

"I'm not either. Hang tight." He yelled out another order and waited. Every precious second felt like an eternity as we waited for the Guatemalan snipers to do their jobs right.

Drones were keeping watch on the property's perimeter from above. Gallardo had been trailed from one of his homes in the mountains to his beachside mansion earlier this morning. Unless the crime boss had an underground tunnel system we didn't know about, he was in that house somewhere. And, for me, success was nothing less than a bullet resting in between Gallardo's eyes. If we escorted him out in handcuffs, he would be out of jail before the ink even dried on his fingers.

Looking off to my left, I saw a cluster of leaves on a banana tree tremble. I flipped the fire selector on my rifle to full-auto, shouldered it, and sent a short burst into the foliage. A young man clutching a grenade launcher fell forward into the grass, dead, his weapon lying beside him.

I rose up just as fresh sniper rounds from our team deterred the gunmen at the front of the building. Cole and I ran toward where the young man's body lay, and I stopped just long enough to grab up the RPG and run for cover on the west side of the building. I heard Cole order his men to our location as I shouldered the grenade launcher. Within thirty seconds half a dozen men were beside us. Cole aimed his assault rifle at a first story window and blew out the glass with an extended burst of fire. Then I aimed the RPG into the house and it shot off with an angry hiss.

It exploded inside the house a moment later, creating a fireball that spread out eight feet in diameter. Cole led the charge into the mansion and I dropped the grenade launcher and followed his team inside.

Painful groans echoed off the tile floors and high ceilings, issuing from men who had been caught in the explosion. As we fanned out, Cole and I moved into the enormous kitchen. A man started to rise up from behind the marble-topped island, and I sent three rounds into his face before his weapon even made it over the counter.

More of our own soon made it inside, and room by room, we cleared each space and began to systematically take down the enemy. Some made it out the back door and fled past the pool and into the backyard toward the hedges that grew tall up against the edge of the beach. They wouldn't get very far; they would be met with another team stationed out on the sand.

With the first floor finally cleared, we advanced up the stairs to the second floor where the hallway forked off into three directions. Cole and I took the one on the far left, followed by three other agents. There were no guards in the hall, which meant everyone was behind closed doors. Coming to the first door on our right, I waited for the team to get in position before flinging it open. We rushed in with weapons at the ready and a woman shrieked—a shrill defenseless cry that sent a shiver through me. Beside her were two young boys. She held a baby girl in her trembling arms.

Gallardo's wife and children.

The monster hadn't even bothered to post a sentry for his own family.

We checked the closet and the room for anyone who might be hiding and searched for weapons before Cole got on the mic, calling for assistance. Leaving an agent in the room to babysit, we continued to the next room on the other side of the hall. The door was unlocked, and I cracked it open to see a shooter at the window, still taking shots at the front lawn. Behind me, Cole updated the snipers on our position inside the house, and then I slipped into the room, stopping only ten feet from the shooter, my muzzle fastened directly on him. "Psst," I said, and he whipped around with a startled expression on his face. I loaded his body with lead before clearing the room and joining the team in the hall. We proceeded through four more rooms, one of them empty, and three with Gallardo's men with their focus out the windows or in the process of reloading.

The door to the last room was different from the others. This was one made of thick steel set into a steel frame. And, of course, it was locked. Special Agent Cole stepped up to the door and rapped loudly, before calling out, "*La gestión interna.*" *Housekeeping.* It was answered by a volley of bullets pinging the door from the inside. Cole flinched back, and I chuckled.

"Guess they have a thing for dirty sheets," I said.

I stepped back and assessed the hallway. From the door to the end of the hall was another twenty feet. On the canary yellow wall hung two paintings of local landscapes and one of Our Lady of Guadalupe. Moving quickly, I removed the pictures from their nails and tossed them to the floor as I murmured a brief apology to the Blessed Mother.

"What are you doing?" asked Cole.

"Getting into that room. Move everyone back."

I used the butt of my rifle to knock the nails up to a steeper angle and then plucked two fragmentation grenades off my rig. I was hoping that the entire wall wasn't made of steel like the door was. We were about to find out. I slipped a grenade on a nail and handed one to Cole, nodding to the naked nail on my right. "Help me with that one," I said.

Cole ordered everyone back into a room and then set the small explosive on the nail. He wrapped his hands around it. "Pin," I said as we tugged out the pull rings. "Ready?"

Cole nodded.

"On my mark. Three . . . two . . . one . . . *mark.*"

We released our grip on the small explosives, and the safety levers flew free and clattered to the floor. Cole followed me into the room where the team was waiting two doors down. I yelled, "Frags out!" and two seconds later the pyrotechnic delay element ignited the explosive filler and the grenades detonated, shaking the room and stirring up a cloud of dust and debris. Gunfire immediately erupted in the hallway. Whoever was in the room was making a last-ditch effort at staying alive.

I looked down at my chest rig and took inventory. I only had one grenade left. Without speaking, Cole unclipped one of his and handed it to me. I exited the room and saw that my plan had been successful. There was a large hole in the wall—a new door to the secure room. Sometimes, you just have to think outside the box. I pulled a pin from the grenade and tossed it through the new doorway, angling to the right. Just before I covered my ears, I heard the panicked voice of someone who knew they were about to die. The detonation erupted, and I shot past the hole in the wall and tossed my last grenade toward the left. As soon as it exploded, I called for the team and led the charge into the room.

I was momentarily disoriented, unable to see anything around me. It was snowing inside the room.

Snowing money.

Benjamin Franklins fluttered in the air and came to rest at our feet and on our shoulders. The entire perimeter of the room was lined with stacks of money running up to the high ceiling.

Two young men lay dead against the wall, their rifles still strapped across their shredded bodies. A fat, heavily bearded man lay on his back near the corner of the room. A blanket of freshly fallen money covered him. I walked up to him and looked down at his broken, bleeding body. He lay there silent and stunned.

"Rico Gallardo. So nice to finally meet you," I said. "I've got to say, I've been in the country for a couple of weeks now, and this is by far the worst reception I've had yet."

He lay sprawled out among millions of dollars, a mountain of cash towering high behind him. I chuckled at the irony and moved some of the money around with my foot. I shook my head. "Can't spend it if you're dead, Gallardo."

The counterfeiter's face was almost unrecognizable; it resembled a nightmarish Halloween mask. A wide piece of shrapnel had cut away a large part of his left cheek. His left eye was gashed in. But he was breathing. And Rico Gallardo breathing was not good.

Cole stepped up beside me. He shook his head and put on a mock grin as he looked at Gallardo's face. "So much for mounting his head on your wall," he said, and then he ordered his team out of the room.

I unholstered my sidearm and pointed it at the crime boss. "Any last words?" I asked him. "Maybe an apology to your wife and kids for leaving them unguarded?"

His eyes burned into mine with a hateful fury. He hocked a bloody wad of spit up at me, but there wasn't enough force behind it and it fell back into his beard.

"My turn." His body shuddered as I emptied all fifteen rounds into him and then sent the toe of my boot into his ribcage. I nodded satisfactorily as I holstered my weapon and then turned to exit the room.

"Where're you going?" Cole asked after me.

"*Cerveza*. The kitchen's downstairs."

CHAPTER THREE

I SPENT the rest of the evening conducting interrogations before finally putting my head on the pillow at just after one o'clock in the morning. A few of Gallardo's security detail had made it through the raid and, now that their leader and his lieutenants were dead, they were a little more willing to speak up and make a deal without having to worry about the safety of their families.

My alarm went off at just after six, and twenty minutes later, I was in a taxi headed to a small airstrip in Escuintla. The Secret Service would be down here for another couple of weeks while they handed off the post-operational reins to the CIA. Gallardo's death would precipitate a power vacuum in the region, so the CIA was stepping in to ensure that his empire was not dispersed into corrupt hands, that it was disassembled altogether.

But my role there was done, so it was time to head back to Florida. I was a special agent for the Federal Intelligence Directorate, Homeland Security's latest addition to their list of more than twenty-five component agencies. The

FID was primarily tasked with a supportive role that brought us into close proximity with the Coast Guard, Immigration and Customs Enforcement (ICE), and the FBI, as we assisted them in high-priority investigations. Most of my work kept me in the general region of South Florida, the Bahamas, and the Caribbean. But sometimes —mostly when I got farmed out to alphabet agencies—I'd end up in places like Guatemala, Panama, or even Colombia. The FID maintained trans-border jurisdiction and, since its inception more than three years ago, had made tremendous strides in keeping Americans safe and the bad guys disoriented.

I was brought along on this particular raid because the Federal Intelligence Directorate had far less oversight than the Secret Service or even the CIA. Homeland wanted to make sure that Gallardo did not make it out of his mansion alive. I was sent along because—should the situation arise—I was the only one who could pull the trigger on an unarmed Gallardo and get away with it.

I said my goodbyes to the team before I left the office early in the morning and invited Special Agent Cole to look me up sometime and said drinks would be on me. He was based out of Miami—less than an hour from my office— and promised to take me up on it. I had liked working with him for a couple of weeks. He was a consummate professional and an easy guy to put your trust in, something important when you're in a firefight.

The taxi pulled up to a packed-earth airstrip that looked like a brown pencil among the surrounding lush green hills. A Dassault Falcon 900LX business jet was already waiting at the head of the strip with the airstairs down. Grabbing my rucksack from the seat beside me, I handed up a generous tip to the driver and wished him well. He didn't look much older than my thirty-five years and by the picture he had taped to the dashboard, he had a wife and four kids to take care of. He brightened when he saw the two one hundred dollar bills I gave him—*not* counterfeit—and thanked me profusely. Most people in the world don't have it nearly as good as those in America, so whenever an opportunity came along to pass along some of the fortune, I did my best to be generous. In just half an hour, he had earned what represented a tenth of the average person's annual income in the poverty-stricken nation.

I got out of the taxi, nodded a goodbye to the elated driver, and then made my way to the welcoming stairs of the aircraft. After a day like the previous one, I was glad I didn't have to fly commercial. God knows I'd done my fair share of it, and I was certainly not above it now. But after taking down a man like Rico Gallardo and spending all night interrogating the tattered remnants of his crew, I needed a couple of hours of quiet to decompress and process before landing stateside. FID would have me back on something new within a day.

Ducking as I entered the aircraft, I said hello to the pilot and copilot and then tossed my ruck on a seat and sat into the one across from it. I fastened my seatbelt as the stairs came up and the pilots performed their pre-flight checks. A couple of minutes later, the engines whined into a stronger pitch and the aircraft lurched forward and pressed me back into my seat as we shot down the runway. There were no attendants on this flight. Just a quick two-and-a-half-hour flight to Miami.

With my right hand, I mindlessly fidgeted with where my wedding ring used to be. I had finally removed it three weeks before. My ring finger still bore the white line from where the sun had failed to touch it for all those years. The ring was in a box in my nightstand at home. I would never get rid of it, I knew, but I had finally come to the point of acceptance by taking it off.

Some days, I felt naked without it. And time still hadn't diminished the pain like I'd thought it would.

I worked my jaw to pop my ears as we gained altitude and soon enough I heard the captain's voice over the intercom. "All right, Mr. Savage. We're at cruising altitude. Please relax and we'll have you to Miami shortly."

That was my cue. I unbuckled my seatbelt and made my way to the couch in the back. I laid down and closed my eyes, crossed my hands over my stomach. The cabin was quiet, almost sounding like the faint whisper of a passing car on a mountain road.

The next thing I knew, my body responded to the slight change in cabin pressure as we began our descent. My eyes flicked open just as the pilot's voice informed me of our arrival time. I stretched out for a few minutes and then returned to my seat.

The wheels were on the ground twenty minutes later, and after thanking the pilots, I stepped into the doorway and to the top of the steps. I closed my eyes and took in a deep breath of Florida's salty, humid air. It was good to be home.

"Oh, come on already!" I heard from below. "I'm hungry."

I opened my eyes to see Brad Pierce, my best friend and fellow FID agent, leaning back against a glistening apple-red Jeep Gladiator—a hybrid truck and Jeep in one. Brad was just under six feet and had blond hair, which he kept in a perpetual high-and-tight, reminiscent from his time in the Corps. He had a strong nose that hooked slightly to the left and piercing green eyes. I made my way down the steps, and he clapped a hand on my back. "You look like you might need a beer."

"Or three," I said and then opened the back door and tossed in my ruck before sliding into the front passenger seat. Brad went around and got in, started up the vehicle, and pulled out. He nodded toward the back seat. "You got his head in that bag, right? You'd better."

"Couldn't get it through customs," I said.

Brad lowered his voice as if Gallardo might be able to hear. "Was he as fat as they say?"

"Fatter. A real tub of guts that guy was."

Brad patted his own growing midsection. "Nothing wrong with that," he said proudly, merging onto the ramp that would take us out of the airport. "The ladies like a little insulation."

"Call it what you will, but you're starting to let yourself go, Marine."

He waved me off. "It's temporary. Just temporary."

I grinned and looked out the window. Brad had been saying the added weight was temporary ever since he had gotten out of the Marine Corps three years before, but each year he added another six or seven pounds to the scale. He wasn't fat—not yet. It was just a slowly expanding midsection.

His last four years in the service had seen Brad doing what many Marines dreamed of: he was a Marine Raider, with the Corps' Special Operations Command—MARSOC. As a special forces soldier, Brad had seen intense fighting in Iraq, rescued hostages in Mali, and assisted in liberating Marawi from ISIS militants. As a Raider, he was one of the best-trained warriors America had ever produced. It was a firefight in the mountains of Afghanistan that finally sent him home for good. A sniper's round shattered his left ankle, and the military doctors were unable to get him combat-ready again. It broke Brad's heart, knowing he would never see battle with his men again, but he was a Marine, and he took the news as best as could be expected.

After several surgeries, Brad's ankle healed up enough so he could pass Homeland's agent physical, and then he joined FID. He still favored his ankle slightly when he walked, but if you weren't looking for it, you'd miss it most of the time. Like any Marine, his posture was always ramrod straight, and he remained a living embodiment of the MARSOC Raider creed: "Always faithful—always forward." That, coupled with a loyalty that went far above what you would expect, made him the best man I know. I was lucky to call him my friend.

We first met on the baseball field in Colorado when we were nine years old, and even though our careers had diverged as adults, we had stayed in constant contact over the years. He was the best man at my wedding and...well, Brad had yet to settle down and stay with a woman longer than three hours.

As we put Miami behind us and began the one hour drive home to Key Largo, I filled him in on the details of the Guatemala mission. Brad was my partner within the FID

—the one who plugged me to their higher-ups and convinced me to join them. He hadn't gone with me to Guatemala because his ankle had started acting up two days before our scheduled departure date. So he was assigned desk duty until he healed up.

In the west, the sun was dying out for the day, bleeding vibrant reds and purples against the darkening horizon as though it were writing its own obituary. I felt my muscles relax the farther south we drove. Living in South Florida, I wasn't much for leaving, and coming back was always sweet.

Taking the Overseas Highway, we passed through Homestead before finally leaving the mainland behind, passing up Barnes Sound and entering Key Largo, the unofficial entrance to the Keys. Brad flipped his turn signal on and turned right at County Road 905, driving a couple more miles before turning into a crushed-shell parking area that carpeted the front of our favorite watering hole. It was generally more locals than tourists, rebels, or renegades, and that suited me just fine.

We got out, and I stretched before shutting my door and heading toward the bar. Above me, palm trees were rustling dryly, and the spirited sound of live music came from the back of the building. There was no shortage of bars on the island, but the Wayward Reef was my hole of choice. We locals just called it The Reef. The building was formed of unpainted clapboard that had grown gray from years under the Florida sun. The simple tin roof was starting to rust in places, and along the front eaves were mounted a couple of plastic dolphins that, oddly enough, looked right at home where they were. The door squeaked a familiar tone as I opened it and walked inside to the loud

clamor of happy conversation and a cover of Bob Seger's
Night Moves. The place was packed to the gunwales, the
loud din of conversation barely rising above the band
playing in the corner. It was a Tuesday night, but it was
March, and the place was filled with Spring-breakers and
snowbirds. No better place to be.

The decor inside was minimal but what was there was
typical. Steel-legged tables and picnic tables filled the
inside floor, and stuffed replicas of mahi, marlins, and a
tortoiseshell adorned the walls, along with a few neon
signs advertising various beers. One shaped like the
Sunshine State. Fishing lines hung between the exposed
rafters with clothespins clipped over them, grabbing onto
iconic vinyl record covers from the '50s to the '80s.
Around here, people were apt to believe that after the
early 1980s, good music died, and I can't say that I
disagree. A shrimping net hung loosely from another
section of the ceiling, and the back of the restaurant had a
metal roller door that was always up when the bar was
open. Tables spilled out onto a deck that merged into a
narrow dock.

I looked across the room and saw an old, round man with
red, glowing cheeks and a snowy white beard behind the
bar. He waved me over with a fleshy hand. Roscoe Green
was about as close as you could get to a real-life version of
Santa Claus. He even donned a suit and played the jolly
old fella for the local kids a night in December each year. I
approached the end of the bar. "You're back!" he yelled.
"How'd it go?"

"It was a success. But I'm always glad to be back." Brad
was the only one who knew exactly where I had been these
last couple of weeks, and why. Roscoe knew who we

worked for, but specifics on investigations and missions were off-limits to anyone outside the agency.

"Good," he said. "Hold on." He grabbed a couple of glasses and filled them with golden liquid from the beer tap. He came back and held them out to me. "You and Brad get started with these. I'll send Amy over in a little while. You'll be out back?"

"Yeah. Thanks, Roscoe." Amy was Roscoe's twenty-six-year-old granddaughter. After working in the New York fashion scene for several years, she finally grew weary of the fast-paced, image-addicted culture up there and moved down to Florida for a slower way of life. That, and to be closer to her grandfather. Roscoe had given her a job as a waitress, and she had quickly become a little sister to both Brad and me. When she wasn't here or spending time with her boyfriend, Amy could be found at the helm of a boat. She loved the water more than anyone else I knew, and she would spend hours in the Gulf exploring new cays and keys, many of which were no larger than a postage stamp.

I turned and followed Brad across the crowded floor and out the back. We walked onto the dock, and the music grew a little quieter as it drifted out of the bar and dispersed across the water. Fishing boats and skiffs were tied off in slips on both sides of us. We found an empty slip and sat down on the edge, our legs dangling off toward the water, and sat quietly like that for a couple of minutes until I looked over and noticed two girls in halter tops and jean shorts heading toward us, each clutching a beer and giggling. They looked to be no more than twenty. They wore deep tans, making me think that they were probably Florida natives—maybe down from Gainesville or Tampa. I was certainly old enough to be a much older brother; in some contexts, I might be old enough to be their father. No thanks. I might have only been in my mid-thirties, but that kind of age gap wasn't in my tackle box. They came and stood behind us. The brunette leaned over near my ear. "Want some company out here?" she asked sweetly.

I sighed and looked off toward the water. Beside me, Brad winced and then looked back over his shoulder. He knew the drill. "Not tonight, ladies. Thanks, though." I'd been told by many that I was a decent-looking dude. Standing tall at six-foot-two, I had a strong jawline and icy blue eyes. Brad thought it was my black wavy hair that sealed the deal. I got hit on just about every time I came to the bar—even when I had my wedding ring on, that didn't seem to bother most of the girls. I was out of season, though. It would be a long time before I was ready to move on. And right now, I didn't think I ever would.

The brunette didn't get the message. "We're only down here for two more nights if you're looking to have some fun." Her tone was more than suggestive.

Looking down at my empty ring finger, I wasn't in the mood for the routine. "Isn't it past your curfew?" I said calmly. "Shouldn't you call your parents and let them know where you are?"

Behind me, I heard an angry huff, and I glanced back over my shoulder. The girl muttered something about me being a jerk before grabbing her friend's hand and storming back down the dock toward the bar.

"Do they keep getting younger?" Brad said, watching them go. "Or am I just getting older?"

"Both. How's the ankle?"

He looked down and rotated it. "Better. I think Kathleen might pull me off the desk now that you're back." He held out an arm and shook his head. "I think I've lost two shades of tan since you've been gone."

Another young woman's voice came from behind us but this one I knew. "Hey, guys! Welcome back, Ryan."

I turned and saw Amy looking down at us. Her hair was naturally blond, but she had recently put pink stripes in it. "Thanks, Amy. How've you been?"

"Awesome. I decided to start working on my online degree, studying marine ecology." She looked out over the water. "I love this place and want to make sure we're taking care of it. You guys want your usual?"

"That would be great," I said. "And that's great about school. If you need any help studying, make sure not to ask Brad. He'll run your grades into the ground."

Brad lifted his glass in a mock toast. "Hear, hear."

Amy smiled and nodded to one of the outside tables. "Looks like a table just opened up. I'll get it cleared and call you over when your food's done."

We thanked her, and she walked away with an energetic bounce in her step.

I drained the last of my beer as Brad spoke up. "I hate to bring this up, but Kathleen is still pissed with you."

I sighed and set my empty glass down beside me. Kathleen Rivers was our boss at FID. "I figured. She hasn't called me to see how things went in Guatemala."

"Yeah," Brad said. "She got all her updates from a Special Agent Cole."

"Well, Cole's a good dude," I said. "I was kind of hoping you would have smoothed things over for me by the time I got back."

He huffed. "I'm not fighting your battles. I'm just glad you didn't drag me down with you on this one. You're lucky she didn't make you ride coach on the way back."

He had a point. "How's the Barker case going?" I asked.

"I'll fill you in tomorrow," he said. "I've made some progress, but we're still missing a connection somewhere. Even the FBI can't nail it down."

Seven weeks ago, Jim Barker, a Miami businessman who owned a commercial trucking fleet, was found murdered in his vacation home on Plantation Key. This was after his business was raided and his trucks were found to be transporting cocaine and marijuana with destinations to Atlanta, Birmingham, and as far away as Denver. After Barker hinted to the DEA that there was more going on within his operation than they knew about, the agency offered him a deal for him to talk. Barker was going to crack something wide open, exposing a stream of revenue that, according to him, had nothing to do with drugs. He had been released on bail and was under house arrest at the time of his murder. Brad and I were given Barker's file when it became apparent that his murder was connected to the information he was about to give up. Someone, somewhere, didn't want him spilling the beans.

I was pulled off the Barker case to go to Guatemala. Now that I was back, my attention would return to the case until we solved it. Like the Federal Intelligence Directorate, the DEA was one of the component agencies beneath the

Homeland umbrella, and the big suits in D.C. wanted to know what Barker was about to give up.

I stood up and grabbed my glass. Brad finished his and handed it up. "Get me another, will you?"

"Sure thing." I went back inside and stepped up to the bar. A television was mounted in each of the two corners. One of them was tuned to SportsCenter, the other to CNN. Both had closed captions on; it was too loud to hear even if Roscoe turned it all the way up. The ESPN was showing highlights from the beginning of March Madness, but it was the newscast that gained my attention. It was displaying aerial footage of Gallardo's Guatemalan compound. The news probably got wind of the raid overnight, and the footage looked like it was from early this morning as the sun was coming up. Federal agents were scattered across the acreage like tiny ants, and military vehicles from the Guatemalan National Army were parked in the circular drive like a child's toy trucks.

There was a lot of fake money in that mansion, but we all knew it wasn't the only place Gallardo kept it stored. What we had seen at the mansion was his personal stash, money that he had slowly and methodically leaked into the system through channels that couldn't lead back to him. The newscaster was saying that it was the largest seizure of U.S. counterfeit since a similar bust in Peru back in 2016. That raid had accounted for more than thirty million dollars' worth of illegitimate bills. I knew the room where I killed Gallardo would have held double that amount. Special Agent Cole and his team would be down there for a long time as they continued an investigation into where the rest of Gallardo's cash was. Once—if—they located it, they would destroy it and move on to the next group of criminals involved in the same kind of dirty business. There was always a next one. Always.

My attention was redirected by Roscoe's gruff voice. "Ryan, that's the fourth time in a row you've upset some young ladies around here." A twinkle entered his eye. "You keep up that streak and I'll have to give you a plate on the wall. Or something."

"Hey, I do my best." I set down the empty glasses. "Let me get a couple more beers."

CHAPTER FOUR

THE BOAT HUMMED QUIETLY AS the young man idled it away from the dock and headed for the open waters of the Gulf. The water was pitch-black, and the dark skin of the sky was punctuated only by pinpricks of distant starlight. He waited until he passed up the channel markers before turning on his running lights. He hated going out late like this. The last time he was certain a Coast Guard ship had seen him. But for whatever reason, they hadn't stopped and questioned him.

Trey Johnson advanced the throttle, and the boat shot forward to twenty-five knots, the wind catching the hair behind his ears and whipping it around his face. A heavy rock of anxiety sat in the pit of his stomach as he angled south and tried to stay calm.

He was sick of this. It had only been a couple of months now, but he was tired of lying to everyone who cared about him. He knew he never should have gotten involved, but he had meant well at first. Now, he just didn't know anymore.

Pushing all such thoughts aside for the next half hour, he kept an iron grip on the wheel until spotting his destination up ahead. The other boat was already there, bobbing gently along a cluster of mangroves. He reduced his speed to idle, threw out a couple of fenders to port, and drew in close.

There were two people on the boat, one of them a huge man that looked like a Mexican bowling ball. Trey had never seen him before and was surprised he didn't sink the boat all on his own. The other man was the same weasel-looking man Trey had dealt with before. He had a pointed chin and a sharp nose. His dark hair was oiled back and it shined off the glow of his running lights. Trey didn't know his name. He didn't know anybody's name. "You have it?" the man asked. Even his voice was shady.

"Yeah. I've got it," Trey said. He had no idea what "it" was, but he did have it.

Without saying a word, Greasy Hair boarded Trey's boat. He stepped up close, reached behind his belt, and pulled something out from the back seam of his shorts. Trey didn't take his eyes off the man, but a shiny glint told him he had produced a knife with a decent-sized blade. Then he shivered when he felt the sharp steel tip press hard beneath his chin, back near his throat. He swallowed hard but didn't move.

"What—what are you doing?" Trey asked through his teeth, trying to stay calm.

"I want to know what *you're* doing," the man said and smiled like an evil cat.

"What do—do you mean?" Trey was a grown man of twenty-six, but he thought he was about to wet himself.

"You staying low, Trey? You make sure you weren't followed?"

Trey was about to nod when he thought better of it: the knife and all. "Yes...and, no. No, I wasn't followed."

"'Cause the rumor is that you might be getting a little tired of the game. You're not getting a little tired of the game, are you, Trey?"

Yes. "No—no, man. I'm in it."

"Good." The knife came away from his flesh, and Trey rubbed at the spot. The man slipped something out of his pocket and slapped it into Trey's hand. He looked down and saw that it was an old flip phone. "Let me have the other one," the man said. Trey reached into the stainless steel cup holder on the dash and grabbed the old phone. He handed it over. "It uses the same charger we gave you last time. Keep it on you. I'll let you know when and where the next pickup is. We won't meet here again. But you need to be available every night this week. I don't know yet when I'll need you to do the next pickup."

Trey felt a panic rise in his throat. "Every night this week?"

The man's face pinched into a deep frown of disgust. "Is that going to be a problem?"

"No—no. I'll make it work."

"Good. You know, you might have been working with us for a bit now, but sometimes I think Barry was wrong about you."

"He wasn't. I'm your man."

"Good." The man suddenly leaned in and put his mouth way too close to Trey's ear. His next words filled the young man with both fury and terror. "Don't forget that we know where you live. At your girlfriend's place." Then he whispered her name.

Trey didn't move, just swallowed hard as the man returned to his own boat. Within half a minute, they had disappeared around the mangroves, and Trey collapsed into the helm seat and put his face in his hands. His mouth was suddenly dry, and he started to wonder just how he was going to get out of all this. *If* he was going to get out of this.

After gathering his nerves, Trey untied his mooring line from the branch. He started the 260 HP MerCruiser engine and idled away from the shallow roots before turning the wheel, hitting the throttle, and charging back home.

CHAPTER FIVE

I woke the next morning to the sun cutting through the window slats beside my bed and the lonely cry of a gull as it coasted over the docks and turned out to open water. I quickly rolled out of bed and knocked out fifty pushups and as many sit-ups. I tried to take care of myself. I'd met too many sea dogs with stiff joints and fuzzy minds, the result of poor diets or over-drinking since their youth. I generally limited myself to three beers or as many pours of liquor in a sitting. Down here, though, there was always cause for exceptions. I thought of my self-imposed alcohol limit as a general guideline, not a hard and fast rule.

I'd spent just over a decade—eleven years, two months—in the military. After basic in Benning and two years at Bragg, I'd joined up with the United States Army Military Police Corps—"Warrior Police"—the branch of the Army responsible for handling investigations, detainee ops, law and order, and sometimes, intelligence operations. Modern-day Warrior Police divisions were a versatile force, which was a necessity these days in a complicated, global world where the real enemy was often hard to distinguish from the innocent, and insurgents were as unpredictable as the wind.

I got out of the service just as the center point of the war had begun to shift. The U.S.'s involvement in the region had become more focused on disrupting the activities of terrorist cells like ISIS and al-Qaeda, as well as training Afghan police and fighting forces to fight on their own, without the need for coalition backup. I would have given Uncle Sam another twenty if I could have. I loved America and all that it stood for. It was not without its warts and shortcomings, but it was the best damn country this planet had ever seen, and I would die for her a hundred times over.

But a different kind of duty had called me away. My grandmother was dying, and it was time for me to repay the generosity and kindness she had selflessly shown me as a boy. My parents had died in a car accident when I was five, and my grandmother patiently raised me and helped me deal with the anger that boiled as the result of losing my parents all too soon. I could honestly say I was the man I was because of her tenacity and strength. Moving back to Denver to be with her, I had taken a job as a weapons instructor at a local range while my wife worked as a NICU nurse at the hospital. My grandmother died a year later, slipping away peacefully in her sleep.

After finishing my last sit up, I stepped into the shower, and within a few minutes, I was out and on the upper deck of my houseboat, sitting in a wooden Adirondack chair and sipping a steaming cup of coffee. I watched as the bright orange orb of the sun punctured the early morning horizon, slowly rising until its light reflected off the water like a million pieces of broken glass, dazzling anyone fortunate enough to see it.

My view each and every morning, and one I never took for granted.

After moving down here from Colorado last year and joining Brad at the FID, I fulfilled a lifelong dream and bought myself a used Gibson 5500 houseboat off an older couple looking to spend the next few years in Spain. The fifty-five-foot boat was equipped with full-sized appliances, three staterooms, two heads, and a walkaround deck. The upper deck had twin biminis, which I generally kept folded back.

When I was a boy, I had been pretty sure that MacGyver was the coolest guy ever, and I don't know that the years have done anything to change my opinion on that. Watching him diffuse a bomb with a paperclip or fix a leaky radiator with a couple of eggs sold me on his status in the Pantheon. He also lived on a houseboat—albeit with no engine—on a lake. Growing up in central Colorado, I'd had no idea you could live on the water like that, so watching Mac step onto a floating house and call it home stoked my seven-year-old imagination and planted a seed that would take nearly thirty more years to finally sprout.

I took a sip of my coffee and waved to a charter captain who was gliding by on the deck of his flybridge. Key Largo is the gateway to the palm-fringed archipelago that is the Florida Keys, more than a thousand islands that span a hundred miles and trickle off the southern tip of the Sunshine state like scattered crumbs. Most tourists use Key Largo as a quick stop on the way down to Key West, but I preferred the closer access to the mainland and a key that didn't have to accommodate cruise ships.

When the sun finally broke away from the horizon, my coffee cup was empty. That was my cue that it was time to head into work.

* * *

THE FID OFFICES were ten miles west of my place, perched on the Gulf side and looking out over Sunset Cove. The two-story building was less than three years old and set in the center of a vibrant green lawn hedged in by royal palms.

I scanned my badge at the front gate and drove my truck into the parking lot. I parked facing the water, and in the distance, I saw a couple of teenagers standing on their paddleboards, gliding over the water like they were in command of the ocean.

The way I see it, every kid should be free to roam around, explore, and see what the world has to offer. But far too many kids these days are busy with their Xbox addictions or completely unable to pull their eyes away from their smartphones to acknowledge a decent sunset. They'll never know the feeling of absolute freedom that comes from taking a skiff out on the water alone or standing at the end of a dock with your line in the water. There's something to be said for being out in nature and disconnecting from technology, even if it's just for a little while.

I put my truck behind me and strolled to the side employee entrance. After scanning my badge I stepped into the air-conditioned lobby. The cool air was welcomed even at this early hour. I nodded a greeting to the security guards and punched the elevator's call button. The security here was contracted out of a federal office in Miami, and for some reason, the guards seemed to switch out every week. I was friendly with them, but keeping up with all their names wasn't going to happen.

To my left was an open flight of stairs. I was partial to such an invention as the elevator, so I always took it. Being out in the field as much as I was, I typically got in enough exercise. Brad, however, was religious in his commitment to take the stairs, I was pretty sure as a simple effort to appease a guilty conscience that constantly chided the former Corpsman for his flabbiness.

The first floor was for support staff, crime lab, and IT, as well as a small office in the back for revolving DEA agents. On the north end was a small weapons armory containing assault rifles, body armor, flashbang grenades, and the like.

I stepped into the elevator and took it to the second floor where the FID agent offices were. The open floor was dotted with desks, cubicles, and, thanks to floor-to-ceiling windows, light that filled the entire space. Looking across the floor, I saw Brad already hard at work. He may have been unhappy about being chained to his desk while I was gone, but the view was something you would see on the cover of a tropical magazine. Our desks looked out onto Sunset Cove and the Gulf of Mexico. It was an enviable view, and I was thankful to have it. It felt like working from the bridge of a ship at port.

"Hey, there's the man of the hour," Brad said as I walked up. He extended his thumb and forefinger and made to shoot me. "Guess who wants to see your ugly mug." He didn't need to tell me, but he did anyway. "The boss lady."

I tossed my keys into my desk drawer and turned toward my boss's corner office. Her door was open and I rapped on it. She looked up at me over the rim of her eyeglasses. "Ryan. Come in. Shut the door."

Kathleen Rose was in her early fifties and kept her graying brown hair dyed a dark chestnut and trimmed to just above her shoulders. She was slim, of average height, and always wore business suits. She was one of those people that you can't picture wearing anything else—like a turtle without a shell. I tried picturing her in a T-shirt and jeans once but synapses misfired. Kathleen was all business all the time, but I liked her. She was in the seat she was in because she knew how to get things done right. And that commanded my respect, even if we butted heads on a lot of things.

I shut the door and took a seat in front of her desk, feeling a little bit like a junior-higher in his principal's office. Kathleen removed her glasses and placed them on the desk. "Congratulations on a successful operation," she said. "The world is already a better place now that Gallardo is dead."

"Thank you," I replied. The air was stiff between us. Apparently I still hadn't made amends for my little mishap last month. And the one the month before that. On the first occasion, I had been following a suspect's car through downtown Miami when he took off and I gave chase. I followed him through five red lights and a school zone before it ended with him losing control and plowing into the north side of Bayside Marketplace. Thankfully, no one but the suspect was injured in the event. My second slap on the wrist occurred after I shot a local drug dealer in the leg for beating his girlfriend's face to a pulp. I admitted the first one was reckless, but that second one... He'd gotten what was coming to him.

Kathleen leaned back in her chair and steepled her fingers. "Ryan, you're an exceptional agent. Even without Brad recommending you to us last year, I would have seen enough merit in you to bring you on my team."

I wasn't sure where this was going or if I should say thanks, so I opted for the safer route and stayed quiet.

"But you continue to show signs of rogue behavior, stepping away from protocol and failing to stand down when ordered." She sighed and I braced myself for a verbal pink slip. "But your performances continue to outweigh the bad. Special Agent Cole with the Secret Service basically sang your praises when I spoke with him this morning. I don't know why, but he likes you." After tapping her fingers on the desk a few times, she said, "I'm going to go ahead and put the past behind us and give you a clean slate."

I felt my muscles relax.

"Make me look good and you've got a friend for life. I don't mind you getting creative and thinking outside the box. That's what investigators are supposed to do. But I need you to stay within the guidelines, even if you don't agree with them. I can't go back to the director and cover your ass again."

"Yes, ma'am. And thank you."

"Good." She said it brusquely, making it clear we were leaving the topic behind. "For now, I want your report on the Gallardo raid on my desk by the end of the day today."

"Today?" I was a notoriously slow typist, having never learned to move beyond just using my index fingers. Ask me to reassemble a multipurpose rifle within a minute and

I'm your man. Put a keyboard in front of me and I'm like a blind chicken trying to peck out a meal.

"Yes," she said. "Will that be a problem?"

Yes. "No," I said coolly.

"I need Guatemala behind us, Ryan. This Barker investigation is taking too long and I need your eyes back on it. Brad will get you up to speed on it tomorrow morning. He's turned up a couple of new connections that look like they're worth pursuing. I need you both to get me something of substance so I can show D.C. that we're not just wasting time down here.

"I'll give it my full attention," I promised. She dismissed me and I went back to my desk. Brad looked over to me, wearing an expectant expression.

"Well?"

"Well...I'm out of the dog house."

"Yeah?" He grinned. "Well, let's see how long that lasts. I kind of like you being in trouble. I'm Kathleen's favorite when she's mad at you."

I sat down and booted up my laptop. Out in the distance, a fishing boat was up on plane as it cut over the calm water at thirty or thirty-five knots. I sighed, entered my password, and started pecking away.

CHAPTER SIX

I DECIDED to skip out on lunch, but my rumbling stomach was saved when Brad returned with a flounder sandwich for me from the restaurant across the street. I was making steady progress with my report, keeping all thoughts of suicide at bay, when my phone rang around three o'clock. It was Amy, but since I was on a roll, I just let it go to voicemail. Half a minute later it rang again. There was obviously some kind of urgency behind her call, so I went ahead and answered it. My aching pointer fingers needed a break anyway.

"Amy," I said. "What's going on?"

"Ryan." Her voice was agitated, worried even. "I know you're at work. I'm sorry to call now but something's going on with Trey."

Trey was Amy's boyfriend. They had been dating for more than a year, and about three months ago he had moved in with her. I liked the kid. He treated Amy well and had a good sense of humor. "What do you mean?"

"He's—well, he's not being honest with me and I'm worried about him. I heard him go out late last night. He thought I was asleep. But he took the keys to his boat."

"You think he's cheating on you?"

"No—no, nothing like that. At least, I don't think so. But he hasn't really been himself for the last couple of weeks. Like he's stressed about something. I can't get him to open up to me. You think you could get away for a few minutes to come talk with him? He may not be around tonight. He was talking about going with a friend to a Marlins game."

I glanced at the time on my computer screen. "Sure. Has Roscoe talked with him?"

"No. Roscoe's out for a couple of hours and I don't want to worry him with this right now." She paused for a moment. "I called Trey and asked him to come to the bar, that I wanted to talk with him.

"Okay." I shut my laptop. "Give me a few minutes. I'll come over."

The parking lot at The Reef was relatively empty when I pulled in. It was midday and most everyone was still in various modes of shopping, fishing, or working. The door gave its familiar squeak as I opened it and went inside.

A white-haired couple was sitting outside enjoying a couple of frozen drinks and Amy and Trey were inside at a corner table, talking quietly. Trey had a slim build and naturally wide eyes that tended to make him look like he was scared all the time. But, for everything I knew, he was a pretty level-headed guy. He and I had always gotten along, and I liked the kid; he seemed to treat Amy well. He made her happy, and that was what mattered most to me. And her grandfather too, for that matter. Although Roscoe had had more than one conversation with me about his concerns regarding Trey's ability to provide for Amy or a family in the long term. Trey worked for a local landscaping company running a lawnmower and a weedeater. It was fine, honest work that anyone could be proud of, but it didn't pay very much, and Trey seemed to have no ambitions to advance in the company or maybe even start one of his own one day. I learned a long time ago that good men don't necessarily make good providers. Sitting there in the corner now, he looked impassive. Amy just looked angry, and I had never known her to get angry very easily. If I had to guess, he still wasn't telling her what she wanted to know.

Trey pulled away from his girlfriend's searching stare as I approached the table. He shook his head and rolled his eyes when he saw me. Then he looked back to her. "So this is why you wanted me to meet you here? Is this like an intervention or something?" His tone was short and cold. I couldn't blame him, though. If I were in his shoes, I probably wouldn't want to talk with me, either. Especially if Amy sprang it on me unannounced.

Without offering a greeting, I said, "Amy loves you, Trey. She's worried about you, is all."

He leaned back in his chair and sighed, looked toward the dock out back. I nodded to Amy and she stood up and returned to the bar without saying anything else. I took her place in the chair and folded my hands on the table.

"Trey," I said quietly, "you know Amy isn't the nagging type. She's got a good head on her shoulders, and she has a pretty strong sense that something's wrong on your side of the tracks. And I'm not sure she's wrong."

"Look," Trey said, shaking his head, "I'm fine, all right? Can't you all just trust me?"

"Generally, I would say yes. But right now you're not giving me a reason to." He looked down at the table. "Trey," I said, "I was an MP in the Army for almost a decade. That means I handled a lot of investigations, met with a lot of people who made some poor decisions. It also means that I can read people. If I thought you were just trying to hide the fact that you got an engagement ring, or that you polished off the last of the ice cream, I'd walk out of here right now. But that's not what it is, is it?"

* * *

AMY BUSIED herself behind the bar while stealing quick glances across the room to gauge how Ryan's conversation with Trey was going. Trey looked stiff as a board. If Ryan couldn't get him to open up, then no one could.

She'd met Trey more than a year ago—he was a deckhand on a deep sea fishing charter she took with her friends. All she had ever known him to be was laid back and chill. He never snapped at her, and she had seen him angry only one other time. And then he'd had a right to be. Someone had keyed the driver's side door of his Camry. But this new development in his demeanor was different. He'd been short with her the last couple of weeks and had become sullen and quiet. About a month ago, she and Trey had started to dabble in discussions of marriage. But surely that wasn't what was bothering him, was it? A voice from behind Amy tore her from her thoughts.

"Who is *that*?"

Amy turned to see Lisa staring across the room at Ryan. Lisa was the newest addition to The Reef's wait staff. Roscoe had just hired her two days ago. She was a striking blonde with bright, lively eyes. "He's not up for grabs," Amy said.

"Why not?" Lisa asked. A playful grin tugged at her lips. "He's a hottie."

Amy slid a couple of clean glasses into the rack above her head. She looked over at Ryan, who was wearing a serious expression while he talked with her boyfriend. "His wife was killed in a car accident two years ago. If that wasn't bad enough, it was only five days after his grandmother died."

"Oh, that's terrible," Lisa said. She looked back to Ryan like now she was seeing him in a different light. "She must have been young."

"She was thirty-two," Amy replied. "And it about split him in two." She looked back at Lisa. "So don't go getting any ideas. He's like an older brother to me."

Lisa put up her hands in surrender. "Okay. Loud and clear."

* * *

Trey's jaw tightened, and he looked off toward the front door, clearly avoiding eye contact with me while silently debating whether to let me in or not. When he turned back to me, I knew what he was going to say before he opened his mouth. "Thanks for coming to talk with me, Ryan. You're a good guy and I appreciate the way you look after Amy." He took in a deep breath. "I just need to figure this out on my own. And if I can't, I'll come to you about it. I promise."

"Trey, if you're into something you shouldn't be, I'm the best person you could talk with about this. Before you end up in handcuffs, or worse."

My offer was answered by the scrape of his chair against the polished concrete floor. He extended a hand and I shook it. "Thanks, Ryan. I really do appreciate it. I've got to get going." And with that, he headed toward the front and walked out the door into the sunlight.

I stood up and went to the bar. No one was behind it, so I pressed myself into a stool and waited. It was oddly quiet in here this time of day. Tropical music played softly over the speakers, but there was no conversation to speak of. When Amy finally appeared out of the kitchen, my presence at the bar surprised her. She raised her chin as she searched the floor behind me. "Did he leave?"

"Yeah."

"Anything?" she asked, almost pleading.

I shook my head. "I'm with you, though. I don't have the best feeling about it. You said he has a boat?"

"Yes. It's a Sea Ray Sundeck. Just a couple of years old. It's the only thing he got from his uncle when he died last year."

"Where does he keep it tied up?"

"At a dock near Heron Park."

"On the Gulf side?" I asked.

"Yes. Why?"

I didn't want to worry her. "Just curious."

"Look," she said, "can we keep this between us for a little while? I don't want to worry RC about it. Not until we have a better idea of what's going on." RC was her nickname for her grandfather. In fact, all seven of Roscoe's grandkids called him RC.

"Sure," I said. "Does Trey have a history with the law? A record of any kind?"

"No," she said quickly. "He's a good guy. You know that."

I did know that. But I also knew that even the good guys sometimes took a wrong turn. "What about financial troubles? Misguided friends?"

She shook her head. "His car is paid off and we rent the house. He's got a monthly note and insurance on his boat. That, and a slip at the dock. It's a nice boat, but it's nothing that's making him stress." She shrugged. "He doesn't have a whole lot of friends."

I went around the bar and gave her a brotherly hug. "I'll keep an eye out. In the meantime don't pester him about it. And let me know if he ends up telling you anything that I should know."

Her face was full of concern. "I hope it's not bad, Ryan. I really do love him."

"I know you do. Chin up."

CHAPTER SEVEN

I HATED PAPERWORK. It was a necessary part of the job, but sometimes I thought I would rather be cleaning stadium toilets after a Super Bowl game than spending hours at a keyboard regurgitating what everyone already knew.

I was shaken from my typing-induced coma by Brad's voice. I blinked and rubbed at my eyes with the heels of my hands. When I looked up, he was standing up at his desk. "I'm leaving," he said. "See you over at The Reef later?"

"Not tonight. Think I'm going to head back home and chill. I'll catch up with you in the morning."

"All righty." Brad grabbed his travel mug from his desk and headed for the door, wearing a mischievous grin. "I hear the old man just hired a new waitress. Think I'll go over and make my acquaintance."

Once the stairwell door clicked shut, I realized I was alone on the floor. Even Kathleen, who usually burned the midnight oil, was gone. The window blinds in her office were open, and her light was off. I spent the next hour finishing up my report on the Guatemala raid. By the time I was done, the shadows outside had grown longer, and a neon sun was touching the horizon. I emailed the finished file to Kathleen and shut my laptop, then looked out over the shimmering water.

I was lucky to live in a place where so many saved their slowly earned vacation days to come visit for just a short time. That, and the fact that I actually worked in a government building that gave its employees a view like this. When I accepted this job, I fully expected to be holed up in a tiny office with drab walls and poor lighting. But when I first stepped onto this floor a year before, I quickly determined it was the best use of taxpayer dollars I had ever seen.

A stunning stretch of the coast this was, but the FID's very existence down here was a testament that all was not well in paradise. These waters and their trail of tiny islands continued to function as trafficking routes for drugs, weapons, and even people. Smugglers, Caribbean pirates, and maritime gangs were as alive as ever, and that knowledge was the primary reason that Brad convincing me to join the FID wasn't such a hard sell. The way I saw it, we were doing the Lord's work on the devil's playground.

My thoughts drifted to Trey and what it was he might have gotten himself into. The possibilities were endless, and after talking with him earlier my radar was blinking like a broken switch.

I stood up and walked across the floor to a heavy metal door, where I scanned my badge on the reader and opened the door, then flicked on the switch to the small room before stepping inside. Metal shelving hugged the walls, and two large metal cases sat on the floor along the back wall: two DJI Phantom 4 PRO drones. Brad and I had used one last month to get video footage of a dockside meeting between a Florida state senator and man suspected of buying state secrets and selling them to the highest bidder. For now, though, the drones were not within my current purview. What I wanted was on the third shelf, next to a rack of night vision goggles.

I lifted the small black case, unzipped it, and folded the top back. Inside were three plastic disks, each the size of a quarter. A device with a glass front rested in a foam insert. It was all there.

I zipped the case closed and passed up the sign-up sheet on my way out. I was supposed to check it out, but I didn't want anyone to know what I was doing. With any luck, I'd have it back in a few days and no one would notice. It was one of those things that would piss Kathleen off, not following protocol, but I was willing to risk it.

I exited the secure room and headed home to grab some dinner and relax until darkness came.

CHAPTER EIGHT

DRIFTER'S DOCK was a couple hundred yards south of Heron Park, on the southern end of Key Largo. It was just after ten in the evening when I glided my truck into a paved parking space and made my way down a narrow boardwalk toward the water. The dock's offices were closed for the night, the place empty, with no one in sight and boats resting quietly in their slips. I took note of a couple of security cameras facing the boats, but I wasn't worried about them. No one would check the feeds unless something unusual was reported, and I planned on getting in and out without being noticed.

There was only one Sun Ray Sundeck among the boats. I quickly slipped on board and squatted down, wiggling my finger into the latch on the cockpit floor and pulling it back. Reaching into my pocket, I produced one of the plastic tracking devices I borrowed from the office and used my thumbnail to remove a thin strip of waxed paper, exposing the adhesive backing. I then placed it on the inside wall of the compartment. It blended well, and even if Trey opened the compartment, he would certainly miss it.

Satisfied, I shut the compartment door and took my leave of the boat. After returning to my truck, I turned on the tracking console and waited for it to boot up. After a minute the small plasma screen pinged the boat's location on the digital map and displayed a strong signal from the tracking device. Using the menu, I set the notifications to alert me when the boat moved away from its current location by more than fifty feet.

I had no idea if Trey was in any trouble, or if he was up to no good. But since he wasn't talking to either me or Amy, it left me having to chart my own course to figure out what exactly might be going on. It was Amy's insistence that he had taken his boat out the night before that had me convinced that this was the best place to start.

With the tracking device in place, I headed back home for what I hoped to be a good night's rest.

* * *

I HEARD my phone ringing in the darkness, sounding far away at first and then increasingly louder the more I came up out of sleep. I didn't wake quite as easily as I did in my twenties, or even a couple of years ago. After my wife died, it just got harder for my body to blink awake like it used to. Groggy, I reached out and felt for the phone. I squinted against the back glow as I looked at the time—1:10 AM. The display showed Brad's name. Sliding my thumb across the glass, I set the phone to my ear. "Yeah?" I said hoarsely.

"Ryan. You awake?"

"Yeah...just finishing my second cup of coffee. What's the deal?"

"You need to turn on the news, man. Like now."

I reluctantly slid my feet onto the floor and sat up. "What's going on?" I stood up and headed into the living room.

"It's Rico Gallardo's mansion. Someone toasted it. It's up in serious flames right now."

I was fully awake now as a hit of adrenaline spiked my veins. "What?" I reached for the remote and turned on the television. "What channel?" It was early in the morning. The Gallardo bust had been big news, but I doubted that all the major news channels were going to interrupt their late-night fringe programming to bring live coverage of it.

"MSNBC," Brad replied.

I found the station and stared at the screen, hardly believing my eyes. An aerial shot was hovering over the massive house I'd been in less than two days before. Angry orange flames were rising out of the roof and licking the sky. The entire property was bathed in an orange glow while third-world firefighters stood idly by, helplessly watching the inferno blaze.

The news ticker indicated that, prior to the blaze, a fire-fight had broken out between the *Policía Nacional Civil* and an armed group of unidentified assailants. I turned up the volume and listened to the newscaster: the fire started two hours ago; how it began was currently unknown; several U.S. Secret Service Agents were injured in the attack—one was killed.

My thoughts immediately went to Agent Cole and his team. In just a short two-week span, I had gotten to know all of them well. They were a great group of professionals who were committed to preserving the financial integrity of our country. I could feel hot anger rising inside me. I still had the phone by my ear. "Have you talked with anyone else?" I asked Brad. "Do we know what happened?"

"I haven't heard from anyone. I'm sure Kathleen will have the scoop in the morning. I was just scrolling channels, thinking about heading to bed when I saw this."

I knew there was probably sixty to seventy million dollars' worth of counterfeit money in that house, that there was no way the Secret Service had finished cataloging and documenting it all. And even if they had, this was certainly not their way of destroying it. There were very strict protocols for how to go about doing that. I also knew a counterfeit one hundred dollar bill could be sold for 30 percent of its face value. That was twenty million just sitting there for the taking. Anyone in the know—someone who worked for Gallardo, a local criminal gang, or even a bad apple in the *Policía Nacional Civil* could be behind this.

My thoughts were jolted by a systematic beeping suddenly coming from my stateroom. I moved quickly across the living room and reached the tracker just as it started to beep louder.

"What the hell is that?" Brad said.

"I need you to meet me here at my dock. ASAP."

"What? Dude, it's like one in the morning."

Trey was on the move.

CHAPTER NINE

BRAD LIVED five miles west of me in a plank-sided bungalow on Plantation Key. Ten minutes after the tracker went off, I was dressed and he was standing on the dock beside my houseboat. I joined him on the dock, and we started toward the other side of the marina, where I maintained another slip with another boat, a Boston Whaler 270 Dauntless. My Whaler included a helm station with an integrated hardtop and a 30-gallon livewell, a fold-down swim patio on the side of the hull, and fore and aft casting decks. It boasted twin 225 Verado engines that, when opened all the way up on calm water, got her up to a steady fifty knots. All said, it was twenty-seven feet of pure fisherman's dream.

Now, you might be thinking how a guy with the meager income of a federal agent who lives on an old Gibson came up with a couple hundred thousand dollars for a kick-ass fishing boat. When my grandmother died a couple of years ago, she left me just over a million-and-a-half clams, completely unexpectedly. I'd never felt the need to live a lavish lifestyle, and there were plenty who had to live without, so after moving down to Florida, buying both boats, a couple of modest rental houses, and setting a little aside for a rainy day, I gave half the inheritance away, split three ways between Wounded Warriors, Monroe County Women's Shelter, and Feeding America. I swear, afterward, I'd never slept so well in my life.

We boarded the Whaler and Brad tossed off my lines. I backed out of the slip. As I idled away from the dock and through the no-wake zone, Brad stood with me in front of the double-wide helm seat. I spent the next five minutes filling him in on the phone call from Amy and the halted conversation with Trey. When I told him I'd borrowed a tracker from the office, a mischievous smile crossed his face. "You're jonesing for Kathleen to fire your ass, aren't you? Using government property for a private investigation?" He shook his head and clicked his tongue. "She finds out about this and you won't even be able to get an investigative job in Podunk, Arkansas."

"Which is exactly why she's not going to find out."

"If you say so. You know my lips are sealed but, I swear, Kathleen is like the upstairs mother who somehow knows when her six-year-old has his hand in the downstairs cookie jar."

He wasn't wrong about that. Still, I cared too much for Amy to let her boyfriend get eaten by sharks, if that's what was even going on. I glanced back down at the tracker and watched as the dot pulsed into Cotton Key Basin, and I gauged that Trey was probably a good eight miles ahead of us. I could only hope that whatever he was doing, I wouldn't be too late to witness it.

My first order of business was getting into the same waters as he was. As it stood now, Trey was on the Gulf side of the Keys and we were on the Atlantic. After getting beyond the markers, I opened up the throttle and headed south toward the tip of Plantation Key, where Tavernier Creek offered us a shallow pass to the other side. Within a few minutes, I slowed on my approach and moved slowly up the inlet, crossing beneath the Overseas Highway before winding through a mangrove forest and coming out into the open waters of the Gulf. Edging up on the throttle, I increased my speed once again and slowly started to gain on the blinking dot. It looked to be cruising at around fifteen knots—the Whaler was doing more than double that. Within ten minutes, I could finally see the Sea Ray's running lights as we passed up the Crane Keys and continued heading on a southwesterly course. I hung back almost a full mile and kept my course on a slightly different degree. Whatever Trey was up to, I could easily imagine him being paranoid about being followed. Novices in crime are typically skittish until they learn the ropes and grow in confidence. Whatever Trey was doing taking his boat out in the middle of the night, he had to be looking over his shoulder every couple of minutes. With the tracker in place, I didn't have to worry about losing him. I just needed to make sure I was close enough to where he docked so I could follow him on foot or get a good line of sight on what was going on.

Finally, the dot started to slow around Panhandle Key, and I altered my course so I could swing around and approach from the opposite direction. "He stopped," Brad finally noted. "We'd better hurry if we don't want to miss what he's up to."

I angled the boat around a couple more islands that were no more than a couple of acres and then eased down on the throttle as we drew closer to where Trey had stopped. Turning off all the lights on my boat, I idled around a cluster of mangroves before turning the boat around and tucking in behind them. From here we would have a clear view of Trey's doings but stay hidden and out of sight. I turned off the engines while Brad grabbed the starboard lines and tied off on the branches so we didn't drift out.

By my estimation, we were a third of a mile from Trey. I had no indication that he'd heard us, and I didn't want to chance getting any closer than that. Sound carries easily over water, and we were already lucky enough that he hadn't heard our approach. Getting any closer could only risk spooking him and possibly make our time out here a complete waste.

Opening one of the storage compartments at the helm, I took out a pair of night vision binoculars I'd brought with me from the houseboat. At my suggestion, Brad had brought his pair as well, and we both set them to our eyes and inspected the situation on the tiny cay.

Trey's Sea Ray was tied up in a similar fashion to ours, nestled along the mangroves and sea grapes. He had turned off all lights except those at his stern. Apparently, he wanted to remain unnoticed. I watched as he took a seat at the bow and ran his fingers through his hair like he was nervous or frustrated. "What are you up to, Trey?" I muttered to myself. Amy's concerned face came into my mind and I felt myself getting angry. Amy was a great girl, and I hated the thought that her guy may have gone off the rails.

A couple of minutes passed before we heard the drone of a strong outboard from the south. A fishing boat came into view and reduced speed as it circled the cay and made its way to where Trey was tied up.

"You see any decals on that other boat?" Brad asked.

"Nope."

The state of Florida required all vessels to affix their assigned registration number and validation decal to both sides of the bow. This boat was running without any decals. That fact alone was risky if you were up to no good. All that had to happen was for the Coast Guard or Sheriff to notice and they had probable cause to board your boat. It was no different from driving a car with no license plate.

The new arrival slipped up next to the Sea Ray, and Trey grabbed one of his lines and tied off on the other boat's cleat. Then he returned to the helm and picked up a back-pack off the deck. He stepped to the gunwale and handed the bag across the narrow slice of water that separated the two boats. The man unzipped it and peered inside, using a small but very bright flashlight.

"This would be a great time to have a night-vision camera," I mumbled.

"Yeah, that would be cool," Brad said. Then I heard a zipping sound beside me. "Here." Brad extended something to me in the darkness. "The power button is right...here." The device turned on and I saw that I was holding a night-vision camera.

I huffed in disbelief. "Where did you get this?"

"You remember Nancy, that hot programmer from San Fran?"

"That redhead you dated for two weeks last year?"

"Yeah."

"I remember."

"This was her camera. She had an amateur photography thing going on. When she left and returned home to California, she forgot to take this one home with her. I never could get her to call or email me back with her address."

"Well, thank you, Nancy," I said and started fighting with the controls.

"The battery is only about half-charged but it should be enough for tonight," he said.

My binoculars had the characteristic green glow that accompanies most night vision. The camera was a standard white monochrome, making it a little harder to see. But it had a good zoom, and I was pretty sure it would get us what we needed.

As I peered into the lens, I adjusted the focus until Trey and his conversation partner were clearly visible. Brad had his binoculars back up too. I snapped off a few shots and waited to get a better view of the other guy's face. In the meantime, Trey was gesturing with his hand in an animated fashion. He seemed pretty upset about something.

"What do you think they're talking about?" Brad said.

* * *

TREY WATCHED as the man unzipped the backpack and looked inside. The creepy-looking man had come by himself tonight—the guy who looked like a bowling ball wasn't with him. "You think I'm going to steal from you?" Trey knew he sounded irritated, but he didn't care anymore.

"No." The man zipped the bag back up. "But then I don't really know you, do I? Lots of greedy people in this business." He dropped the bag at his feet and returned to the helm of his boat. "Tomorrow night. Same time."

Three nights in a row? "Look," Trey said, "I think I'm done with all this. It's just not going to work for me anymore. I probably shouldn't have gotten involved in the first place."

The man wasted no time redirecting the beam of his flashlight into Trey's face. Trey put up a hand to block the glare and looked away. "What did you just say?"

"I said I want out. This is more than I thought it would be when I started. Barry said it would just be a drop off a couple of times a month and I could quit whenever I wanted."

"Did he now? Barry said that?"

"He did."

"Well, Barry's a liar. I'm sorry you didn't know that when you signed up. But this here? This is a one-way street. You can come down it as far as you want but there's no going back up. You're saying you want to go back up?"

Trey didn't answer. He suddenly felt very nervous and short of breath.

"I need to know," the man pressed. "You're wanting out of our arrangement?"

"No—no, it's fine. I'll keep it up."

The man shook his head and reached into a cup holder and brought out a pack of Marlboros and a lighter. He slipped out a cigarette, stuck it between his lips, and lit up. He sucked in a lungful of smoke and shook his head as he blew it out. "Barry may not have been honest with you, but I will be. Hearing you say that makes me nervous. Do you know what happens to people who want out? Who think they can just walk away?" He took another long drag.

"No. What?"

"A lot of times they suddenly recover their moral compass and go running scared to the police. You catch my drift?"

"I'm not one of those guys."

"So they all say."

It was silent for a while, Trey not knowing what to say and the guy continuing to work on his cancer stick. Finally, he flicked it into the water where the orange glow at the tip died with a brief hiss. "Tell you what," the man said. "You do one more run for me and I'll let you off the hook. You seem like a pretty decent kid. I'll talk to Barry about getting the facts right from now on when he pitches the job to someone."

Trey felt like a load of bricks had just slipped off his back and into the water. "Yeah? That would be great."

The man started to unravel his lines from the Sea Ray's cleat. "Tomorrow night," he said again. "Right here. Two AM. That work for you?"

"Yeah—yeah, that's fine."

"Good." The other boat growled to life, and the guy gave Trey a brief two-finger salute before backing away and shooting off into the blackness once he got clear.

CHAPTER TEN

I DIDN'T GET my head back on my pillow until nearly four o'clock, and my concerns over Trey and the Secret Service team in Guatemala kept me hovering in a half-sleep for a couple of hours. I finally got up around six and took a hot shower before taking my coffee up to the top deck and watching the world wake before going back down to retrieve my cell phone. I tried calling Agent Cole a couple of times but it went straight to voicemail, so after sending him a text, I just decided to head into the office a little earlier than usual. I had barely gotten into my Ram and pulled away from the marina when Kathleen called me.

She didn't bother with a greeting. "Ryan, did you hear?"

"Yeah. We've got some good people down there. Do we have any idea what happened?"

"No. But I'm in the car heading up to Miami. I have a meeting with my boss to discuss it. I've already got a couple of calls into the Secret Service for you. As soon as I hear something you'll be the first to know."

Kathleen and I had our differences, and most of those were my fault, but I was glad I reported to her. She always had our backs when it mattered and understood what it meant to go out on a limb for someone on the team. "Thanks, Kathleen. I'm heading into the office now."

"I should be back around lunch. In the meantime, you and Brad try to make some progress on the Barker case. There's something there. We just need to find out what or who it is."

We hung up and I drummed my fingers on the steering wheel all the way to the office. I felt myself getting angrier with each passing mile, wishing I had been at Gallardo's mansion last night. At least then I could have taken out a few more of the a-holes that assaulted my fellow federal agents. I may not work for the Secret Service, but at the end of the day, we're all just trying to do the same thing: keep our country safer. When you work alongside someone for fifteen hours a day for two weeks straight and then spend most every night drinking third-rate mezcal and swapping war stories, you tend to see them as a brother in arms.

Getting to my office, I went up and sat at my desk before realizing that I didn't really have anything to do. Brad wasn't in yet, and I hadn't been brought up to speed on the investigation. So I spent the next hour checking and responding to some emails and refreshing myself on the details of Jim Barker's murder. Finally, I heard Brad step out of the stairwell humming "Achy Breaky Heart" about as loud as a grown man can.

"Man, you've got to get a new tune."

"What? No way."

"You have the camera?"

He tapped a black canvas bag slung over his shoulder. "Right here. Actually, I transferred the images to a USB drive. I just stopped by Krugman's office but he had a note on his door saying that he won't be in until around ten this morning." He set the bag down at his feet and then sat down and flipped open his laptop before glancing back toward Kathleen's office. "Where's the boss lady?"

I filled him in on my brief conversation with Kathleen and then said, "So, what's new with the Barker case?"

* * *

As it turned out, while I was gone Brad had made some definitive progress on identifying Jim Barker's network of black market contacts, which was the FID's primary interest in the case. Crucial information had died with Barker, information that pointed beyond just moving dope, and we were tasked with finding out just what that was.

Between connections to Barker's truck drivers, supervisors, and a banking transaction that led to a known crime syndicate in the Bahamas, it looked like we were finally getting somewhere. "And, look at this," Brad was saying. "While you were sunbathing down in Central America, I kept coming across this dude named Eric Scahill. He's your typical sewer rat, but he's super well-connected into the underworld. I wouldn't be surprised if he's the middle man, the one who got Barker's trucking company connected with the cartels looking to move their dope further into the U.S. That, or Scahill could have pitched a completely different source of revenue. Either way, if we can bring him in for questioning, I'm sure he'll give us something good."

"Why haven't you brought him in yet?"

"Because right after Barker was killed, Scahill flew the coop. He just up and disappeared."

"What makes you think they didn't get him too?"

"Because," Brad said, "we have a credit card transaction from him a week after Barker's murder. A gas station in Orlando. CCTV confirms it was him. But after that...nada. He's a ghost. A very nervous ghost, I might add. He's running from someone."

I fumbled through the small stack of dossiers he'd given me. "You know, this is why they invented cork boards and string. So we can see the bigger picture."

"Nah, I like it this way better. I don't have time to play with string. I'm not a cat."

I found the page I was looking for and pointed to the picture of a man with large ears and a wiry mustache. "What about Townsend? It says here that during questioning he admitted to knowingly moving dope on his big rig."

"Yeah, but the DEA's already flipped him, and they're confident he's given up everything he knows. And that only leads back to a pot grower in Mexico. Nothing they didn't already know."

I kicked my feet up on my desk and laced my fingers behind my head. "So what do we have other than Scahill?"

"I'm still waiting on Kathleen to see if she can get access to one of Barker's accounts in the Caymans. But she's not very optimistic about that. That would open up a whole new world." Brad shook his head. "We're still missing a piece. I just can't see which one it is." He waved a hand across the paperwork. "But it's in here somewhere."

We spent the next couple of hours sifting through files on more than a dozen persons of interest, cross-referencing them with known offenders already in our system. When I finally looked up and noted the time, I saw that it was after ten o'clock. "Hey, Krugman should be in by now."

Brad leaned back in his chair and stretched his arms as he let out an extended yawn. "You kept me out too late last night. I missed out on my beauty sleep."

"You'll need a lot more than a few hours of sleep to make that face look pretty. Come on." Brad stepped away from his desk and followed me down the stairs to the first floor, where we took the main hallway to the end and tried the door handle to the lab. It opened, and we stepped inside. Stainless steel tables and Formica countertops were filled with microscopes, test tubes, soldering irons, and all kinds of gadgets in various stages of testing. On the far wall were half a dozen computer screens displaying readings and data that made absolutely no sense to me. The FID lab had a federal budget to work in conjunction with top government researchers around the country to create and advance new technologies that agents could use in the field.

Dale Krugman was the lab's director and probably the smartest person—and shortest adult—I've ever met. If I said he was an inch over five feet, that would probably be generous—a brilliant man in a ten-year-old's body. His blond hair came out of his head in tight, curly locks, and rose up high around his head. It looked like a yellow afro. Between his hair and thick-framed glasses that made his eyes look twice their size, he had that mad scientist kind of look. Except he wasn't your typical absent-minded professor. He never forgot a thing and if you asked him to do something for you, it was always done in a timely manner. Krugman could have gone into the private sector and made ten times what he was making here, but he didn't because he wanted to put his abilities to work directly for his country. What he and his team created here in the lab could be developed and put into use in the field much faster than some of the technology development by private companies, who typically had to go through lengthy approval processes.

Brad and I stepped around a table filled with what looked like metallic spiders and I heard Krugman before I saw him. "Well, there's the dynamic duo. What do you guys have for me?" He appeared from behind a large metal contraption in the center of the floor. I'd never seen it before. It looked like an x-ray machine.

I looked down at him as he approached. "How's the weather down there, Krugman?"

"I've got more than one kind of Taser in here. Want to see how they feel?"

"Ryan's sorry for the comment," Brad said. "He's just feeling *shorted* by something Kathleen said yesterday."

Krugman put his hands on his hips and looked at us like an agitated mother. "You both done? Got it all out of your system?"

I looked over at Brad and shrugged, then back to Krug-man. "Yeah. All right. We're done. For now."

"What do you have?"

Brad had downloaded the pictures we had taken the night before to an external drive. He drew it out of his pocket and handed it over. "We took some photos with a night vision camera last night. We need to identify a man and wanted to see if you can run it through FPL." The Federal Photo Library housed more than a billion photographs. It was used primarily as a means to identify suspects and their networks.

"Of course."

"You'll see two people in the photos," I said. "One is a blond guy. We already know who he is. We're interested in the other guy. Dark, slicked back, oily hair."

"Perfect." Krugman smiled. "They're running updates on the system right now, but I could probably get you some-thing by the end of the day if your guy is in there."

"You think you might be able to keep this on the down low?" I said. "It's more of a personal angle we're running on something."

Krugman raised his brows. "You mean, you want me to use government resources on a personal investigation that has nothing to do with the security of your country?"

Brad looked off into a corner. "Yes...?"

"Okay," Krugman nodded. "But if I do this for you then no more short jokes for the rest of the month."

"That's a tall order." When the scientist failed to return his smile, Brad said, "Okay, fine. No more jokes about your malfunctioning pituitary for the rest of the month."

At that, Krugman looked pleased. I jutted my chin toward the x-ray machine. "What's that you're working on?"

Krugman smiled like an evil industrialist. "Come on, I'll show you." We followed him over and he extended a hand. "This here, gentlemen, is a frequency pulmonator, or an FPM. Now, it's just a prototype. Once it's finalized and built to scale, it will be about a tenth of the size it is now, no larger than a weekend ice chest. And much lighter."

I stepped around the machine, where an LED display showed a dynamic graph chart. "What's it do?"

"It's intended to assist in boat chases. The FPM will sync with a boat's frequency—whichever one you have it latched on to—then it confuses the engine's computer with a frequency of its own and causes the engines to misfire, shutting them down. We tested it on the water a couple of days ago but had to call the Coast Guard. Damn thing malfunctioned and shut down *our* boat! I couldn't get the engine started again."

Brad shook his head. "So you're saying it shorted out."

"We had a deal!" Krugman snapped.

"Yeah, but you haven't done what I asked yet."

Krugman sighed. "You two get out of here and let me work."

"Fair enough," I said. "Let me know when that FPM is ready for use. That could certainly come in handy."

"Will do."

We thanked him and as soon as we left the lab and stepped into the hallway, Brad's phone dinged in his pocket. He pulled it out and a smile spread across his face. "Scahill just used his credit card. A motel down in Islamorada."

I turned down the hall leading back to the front entrance. "My truck or yours?"

CHAPTER ELEVEN

ISLAMORADA WAS twenty minutes west on the Overseas Highway. It was famous for beautiful sketches of reefs that made it a diving and snorkeling paradise. I pulled my truck into a parking space at the front of the Mahi Motel, and Brad and I went inside and approached the front counter.

The tiny reception area smelled like stale cigarette smoke, and the faded turquoise walls looked like they hadn't seen a paint job since before Jimmy Buffett was born. The old lady behind the counter had a cigarette stuffed between her lips, and her graying hair was tucked behind her back in a thick braid. Her fat breasts spilled out of a tank top, showing off a wrinkled tattoo of what may have, at one time in the very distant past, been a heart. Even Brad, who was generally not too choosy when it came to cleavage, was repulsed by the sight. She was watching some show on her phone that involved a lot of angry people yelling. I introduced myself and extended my badge over the counter. "You had a Stephen Scahill check in about an hour ago. We need to know what room you put him in."

She leaned back in her chair and frowned. After taking in a lung full of smoke and blowing it out in a thin haze, she said, "You got a warrant or something?"

"I don't need a warrant. We're not searching anyone's room. I just need to knock on his door."

"I'm fairly certain that you need a warrant for something like that. I can't give you a room number without a warrant."

Brad shot me an exasperated look. She was going to make me play hardball. "Look," I said, "I'm not trying to interrupt your day or keep you from watching Jerry Springer, but if this is how you want to play it, then fine. I happen to know that the Sheriff has to send a deputy over here at least three times a week for domestic disturbances, very often there are ladies hanging around that don't do the kind of tricks a magician does, and local pushers of fine white powder tend to lie low in your fine rooms. So, that being the case, I'm bound to file Form 383 with my office. Do you know what Form 383 is?"

"No," she said, looking slightly concerned now.

"It's what Homeland Security refers to as the Location Complicity Form. Basically, what that means for you is that the federal government will have your motel under suspicion for providing refuge to drug dealers and prostitutes."

"We don't have none of that here," she growled.

"Be that as it may, we won't be sure until a thorough investigation takes place. And right now that would take quite a while. We're really backed up and might not get around to clearing the motel to resume business for what"—I looked to Brad—"a month, maybe more?"

"Probably more." Brad nodded. "Very backed up right now."

The old lady swore under her breath and ran her finger over a ledger in front of her. "He's in...110. On the other side."

I smiled. "Thank you. That's all we needed." Her eyes burned into my back as we walked back into the fresh air.

"Form 383." Brad chuckled. "Good one."

Part of being a good agent was making up stuff on the spot that suits your purposes. All she needed was a little scare, and I was happy to invent one. We walked across the parking lot and past the front run of rooms, the air conditioning units rattling loudly. I heard a door click shut just before we turned the corner. We started scanning door numbers. My sidearm was a Glock 21, chambered in .45 ACP, and I drew it from its holster as we arrived at room 110. Behind us an old Toyota Corolla was ticking like it had just been turned off. I turned back around and glanced at Brad. Seeing that his weapon was at the ready, I raised my hand to knock just before a blood-curdling scream reverberated from the other side of the door.

CHAPTER TWELVE

BEFORE THE SCREAM had fully trailed off, my free hand was on the door handle. It was locked, so I stepped back and as Brad slid in beside me, I sent three rounds into the wooden door frame. The best scenario on the other side of the door was that a skittish woman had just found a cockroach crawling across the television screen. But possessing the knowledge that a former convict had just booked the room left me unwilling to take any chances. I would rather explain to Kathleen why I busted into the room of a woman scared of a bug, and not why I failed to act given what I knew going into the situation.

The .45 ACP packs a punch, and the report echoed loudly in my ears as I brought my gun up and stepped back. Brad moved in front of the door and, with his own weapon drawn, lifted his knee and kicked in the door at the lock plate. The splintered wood gave way, and the door swung open as we charged in.

At the end of the room, a woman was sitting against the wall with her head tucked between her legs and her hands over her ears. Ignoring her for the moment while we cleared the room, I immediately noticed the door to the adjoining room was open and that it was dark over there—all the lights were off. I moved past the woman, who was now staring up at me with shaking hands and terrified eyes. When I pushed open the bathroom door, I saw what all the fuss was about. Fresh, bright blood smeared the walls of the shower stall, and a man's naked body lay lifeless in the tub. His body was wet and he still had shampoo lathered in his dark hair. I quickly stepped out of the bathroom and just as I turned to the woman, I heard the patter of urgent footsteps outside. Something seemed to click behind her eyes because she raised her hand and pointed toward the front door.

"Him." Her voice was barely a hoarse whisper. "That's...him."

Brad had just stepped into the adjoining room with his gun out in front of him when I darted toward the front door. "Stay with her!" I yelled and ran out into the parking lot. Twenty yards away I saw a slender man in shorts and a light brown ski mask booking it toward a rusted chain-link fence at the end of the parking lot. I reholstered my Glock as I pumped my legs and tore down the pavement after him. Within seconds he'd scaled the fence and was running toward the back of a strip club.

I reached the fence and had no problems getting to the top. Once there, I momentarily balanced with both feet and then dropped to the pavement. I put on as much speed as I could muster and skirted the back of the strip club. Coming around the front, I was about to ask the day bouncer if someone had just run inside when he saw me and quickly made a connection. Lifting his arm, he pointed across the street. "Went that way," he said. I raised a hand in thanks as I passed and could only hope he was telling the truth. An SUV laid on its horn and I barely missed getting clipped as I bolted across the street and entered a single-street neighborhood that sat near the edge of the water.

Retrieving my Glock again, I crept between two houses and moved through a lush backyard before passing into a forest of sea grapes that grew up along the water's edge. I turned so I could scan the backyards. I knew he was out here somewhere, but where, and what direction he'd gone was still unclear. After waiting half a minute for any movement in the backyards or a sound in the forest, I moved farther into the sea grapes, my gun at the ready and my ears perked for any sound that might send me in the right direction. The sea grapes thinned out into a sandy area spotted with palm trees and the occasional mangrove. I stayed in the shadows as I moved. The sun was still high in the sky, but some cover was better than none. All I could hear was the dry rustle of palm fronds and the gentle lapping of the water until, through the thick vegetation, I heard the familiar drone of an outboard rev up. My adrenaline spiked as I realized that I was further away than I should be. I retraced my steps and ran the opposite direction from where I'd entered the beach. The motor grew louder as it was fed more gas. It was another ten seconds before I burst out onto the open sand and saw a skiff heading out into open water. The operator was looking back at me, his ski mask still on. He sat on a bench seat at the stern, one hand on the tiller, the other raised in the air giving me the bird. My blood boiling, I brought out my gun, aimed, and started to squeeze the trigger before lowering it and kicking at the sand. The effective fire range for a Glock 21 was fifty-five yards. He was double that as it was. I found a large rock on the edge of the water and flung it down in anger. I couldn't believe I let him get away. He had just taken out the one strong lead we had. And now whoever he was, he was gone too. I retrieved my phone and called the Coast Guard. With any luck, they would grab him before he could get too far. But out here there were dozens of tiny keys off the coast he could hide in before darkness fell.

* * *

By the time I made it back to the motel, the parking lot was full of emergency vehicles and cordoned off with crime scene tape. I showed my badge to the deputy at the perimeter, and he lifted the tape so I could pass through.

Brad was talking with a deputy and excused himself when he saw me. "What happened? You get him?"

I shook my head.

"Really? Damn. I've never known anyone to outrun you. You feeling okay?"

I looked toward the open door of Scahill's room. "You figure out what happened here?"

"Well, we got here right on time. Scahill was taking a shower when he was murdered. The woman is—was—his girlfriend. Della Gleason. She checked into the motel with him and then left to go get a few groceries. She had just gotten back when we showed up. The scream was her finding the body and as soon as she turned around she saw the killer pointing a gun right at her. It was her screaming that made him hesitate and then run out through the other room."

"Who checked into the room next door? Or did Scahill have that one too?"

"No. I've already talked to that lovely lady at the front desk. Even after hearing that there had just been a murder on her property she still seemed irritated that I was trying to talk with her. I think maybe I was interrupting *Trailer Park Boys* or something."

"So who was in the other room?"

"Some guy who booked room 111 and paid cash about fifteen minutes before we arrived."

"She say what he looked liked?"

A grin spread across Brad's face. "Yep, and that's the best part. Wanna guess?"

"Guess—?" Then I got it. "Please don't tell me that she said he booked a room while wearing a ski mask."

"Indeed. You believe that? And she didn't seem to care a nickel about it."

"Only in Florida," I muttered. "Unbelievable. He probably paid her ten bucks and fed her a few lines to regurgitate."

"I think that's exactly why the SO plans on bringing her in for questioning."

"How did the adjoining door get unlocked?"

"With a combination of lock picking tools, strong magnets, a taut wire that looks something like a coat hanger, and a tiny mirror. He came prepared." He nodded toward one of the crime scene techs. "They've got it all bagged. Might be able to pull some prints off it all, but I doubt it."

This entire case was a jumbled mess, but it served to make clear that Scahill had known something. Starting with Barker's murder, someone had been diligent in covering their tracks, ensuring that no one could yank them from the shadows.

Brad said, "Either someone had the means to keep an eye on his credit card transactions too or they finally caught up with him and followed him here."

I looked over the crowd of deputies and first responders. "Where's the detective?"

Brad stuffed his hands in his pockets and pointed with his chin. "That's him over there. Detective Wallace. A real baby-faced gem."

I followed his gaze to a young man who looked like he had barely started shaving. He wore dark slacks and a white polo. He was in the middle of a conversation with a deputy when he saw Brad approach with me at his side. He rolled his eyes, but I still extended my hand and introduced myself.

He didn't bother to take my hand. "I've already told your partner that you're not talking to my witness."

I wasn't in the mood for this. I tried to operate with the understanding that most of us are just trying to do the best we can with what we have. The detective was just doing his job. Maybe his attitude had to do with a fight he'd had with his wife before his shift, or maybe he'd screwed up his last couple of investigations and needed to get this one right.

"I appreciate you operating a tight ship, Detective, but my partner and I were here tonight on an investigation of our own. Miss Gleason is now a person of interest to us, and I need to speak with her. Immediately."

"Your investigation is of no concern to me, Mr. Savage. I've never even heard of your agency. If you need anything else, you can call and speak with my boss." He turned and went back into the motel room. Inside, camera flashes blinked as the crime scene unit documented the room.

I pulled out my phone and punched a number in my contacts. "You calling his boss?" Brad asked.

"Nope. I'm calling mine."

CHAPTER THIRTEEN

AFTER I GOT off the phone with Kathleen, Brad and I only had to wait another three minutes before Detective Wallace reappeared in the doorway and headed toward us. He had the look of a man who had just gotten his ass chewed out. He cleared his throat. "Look, I'm sorry about earlier," he said. "Miss Gleason is over there. Take all the time you need."

I thanked him and made my way over to an ambulance with its back doors open. Della was sitting on the back bumper. She was pretty but had a dazed look in her eyes. Her black hair was pulled back into a ponytail, and mascara had tracked down her face like dirty tears. I introduced myself and asked if I could speak with her about what had happened in the motel room. She answered with a weak nod of her head. "I already answered some questions for the detective."

"Understood. But we're with a division of Homeland Security."

"Am—am I in some kind of trouble?"

"No, at least, not as far as I know. We all just have a lot of questions, and we're trying to get a handle on what happened."

"Okay."

"Can you start with how you knew Mr. Scahill?"

"We met at the Clam Shell in Marathon. I had just broken up with my boyfriend when I met Eric at the bar. We hit it off and have just been roaming between Tampa and Miami and the Keys for the last couple of months." She got a faraway look in her eyes. "It was a lot of fun."

"How long ago did you two first meet?" Brad asked.

"About five weeks ago tomorrow. I remember because it was the day after my birthday."

That explained why she hadn't shown up as a possible connection to him. Scahill must have made his way down here after he was last seen at the gas station in Orlando. "Did he ever say anything to you about his past? About things he may have been involved with?"

A frown creased her brow. "No. Not really. He told me he used to sell cars for a living but got tired of the nine-to-five and wanted to live a little. We didn't talk a lot about our pasts. Just about stuff we wanted to do together and the things we had already done." Up to this point, she had been staring at the pavement. Now she looked up at me. "Why? What'd he do?"

"Eric was wanted as a person of interest in a murder investigation in Miami. He wasn't seen as a suspect."

She sighed heavily. "After a while, I started suspecting that he was probably running from somethin'. I just never wanted to know from what. I was having too much fun."

"Why did he use his credit card here at the motel?" Brad asked. "He hadn't used it in several weeks."

A heavy look of shame passed over her face. "Because my cards all hit their limit. I had some cash that I'd been saving, and that held us up for the first few weeks. But, you know that kinda thing don't last forever and it ran out. He said using his card just this one time should be fine."

"Della," I said, "is there anything else you can remember? Did he ever call anyone or did he mention something that didn't make sense at the time?"

"No, not...really." When she blinked next, it looked like she had just recalled something. But she stayed silent.

Brad saw it too. "Nothing?" he said. "Della, if you know anything we're the only people that are fully invested in finding his killer."

She hesitated, started to speak, and then halted. Finally, "He kept an empty can of Diet Coke on the floorboard of the car." She blurted it out quickly, like she was being forced to give up nuclear codes to the enemy.

Brad and I exchanged glances. "Coke can?" I repeated. She'd been through a lot in the last half hour. It was looking like she had hit her limit.

"Yes. He said he had some important information and that when the time was right, he would get a lot of money for it."

"And what's the Coke can have to do with that?"

"Well, that's where he kept the information." What she was saying still made no sense. She looked up at us and seemed to finally understand that. "Sorry. It's a USB port or drive—or whatever those things are called. My car is twenty years old and no one's going to steal it. And it's as sure as hell that no one is going to clean it out. So he kept it there so he wouldn't lose it while we were traveling.

I looked back to Brad who seemed as shocked as I was. It was actually a pretty damn good idea.

"Do you have your keys on you?"

"Yes." She stood up and dug them out of her pocket.

"Would you mind getting it for us?"

She nodded and we followed her to her car. She unlocked it and opened the back door, reached down, and plucked a dented can of Diet Coke from a scattering of empty packs of cigarettes, torn candy wrappers, and old newspapers. "Here." She held it out to me.

The tab was missing and because of the dent, I couldn't see in the back. I shook it but nothing sounded inside. "You sure that—"

"He glued it down in there. You'll have to cut into it."

With my keys, I punctured a hole in the side and wedged the key back and forth, praying to God I didn't slice my finger off. I pulled the key out and used both hands to tear the can apart. There, as Della said, was a dark grey USB drive attached to the inside of the can.

"Well, looka that," Brad said.

I worked it off the aluminum, and it popped free just as Detective Wallace stepped back outside and came toward us. "What are you doing?"

I palmed the USB drive so that it was out of sight. "Just found an old soda can by her tire. Trying to be a good citizen. I don't like trash."

"Don't litter, it makes the world bitter," Brad quipped.

Wallace shot him an angry glare and then walked away again. We thanked Della for her time and went back out of the perimeter. I flipped my keys in my hand. "Come on. Let's get back to the office."

Brad fell into step beside me and shook his head. "It was a simple foot chase. Can't believe you let him get away."

I wanted to punch him, but didn't.

CHAPTER FOURTEEN

KATHLEEN GOT to the office a couple of minutes before we did. She was talking to a secretary when we walked onto the floor. She was clutching her briefcase, and her suit jacket was slung over her arm. Seeing us across the floor, she waved us into her office. We followed her in and plopped into the two seats in front of her desk. "You both don't know how to stay out of trouble, do you?" She said it lightheartedly as she sat into her chair.

Brad raised his hands in defense. "It was Ryan. He was complaining about being bored and said we should go find a super fresh murder."

Kathleen folded her hands in front of her and leaned forward. "So what happened?"

We filled her in on the transaction notification that led us to the motel and what occurred as we arrived. Brad made sure to express his disappointment yet again that I hadn't grabbed the guy.

Kathleen eyed his midsection from her place across the desk. "Brad, I think if either of you could have caught up to the murderer, it would have been Ryan."

He looked down and patted his stomach. "It's okay," he said to it. "Don't let them get to you."

I held up the USB drive with a smile. "The girlfriend gave us this. Scahill told her there was some good info on it. I think we've got a fresh trail to sniff."

"Did she say what was on it?"

"Nope," Brad said. "But as soon as we get back to our desks, we're going to find out."

"How did Miami go this morning?" I asked her.

Brad grinned. "I just bet you love talking with all the professional brown-nosers who get to wear suits all day."

"Those brown-nosers, as you call them, are actually fine men and women who, for whatever reason, choose to keep you on our payroll." Her tone was sharp, but her eyes were softer. Deep down, in spite of all the grief we gave her, I knew that Kathleen loved us.

"Tell me you have some good news about Guatemala," I said, but the sudden tightness in her jaw told me otherwise.

"I wish I did." She pushed her seat back and crossed her legs. "It appears that a Central American crime syndicate by the name of *Halcón Negro* was responsible for the attack on Gallardo's mansion last night. The Secret Service and the CIA had some of their own watching the perimeter as well as some officers from the *Policía Nacional Civil*. *Halcón Negro* assembled more than a hundred men to attack the property. Our people were overrun and had to pull back into the jungle. The counterfeit money was stolen and then they set fire to the mansion."

So someone made out with more than thirty million dollars. Not a terrible payday, although it was going to take them a long time to sell it all off on the street. "The news last night said that someone from the Secret Service was killed?"

"Yes," she said. "A Robbie Stanton."

Brad studied my hardened expression. "You knew him?"

"Yeah. This was his first assignment overseas. He had a young wife and a newborn baby."

Kathleen continued. "Ryan, I know you worked closely with Special Agent Bud Cole during your time down there. He received minor injuries on his back but took a round in the shoulder. He's on his way back to Miami now, along with the rest of his team."

"Those bad guys down there are like Whac-A-Mole," Brad said. "You take one out and another pops up right away to take his place."

"That's why the CIA was there," I said. "To make sure the organization around all that money was disassembled. But this sounds more like a cut and dry robbery, albeit highly organized."

"The CIA is completely taking over things down there," Kathleen said. "Needless to say it's not the best day for the Secret Service."

My phone rang in my pocket and Kathleen dismissed us as I pulled it out. The call was from Amy, and Brad followed me out as we headed back to our desks. "Hey, Amy." I sat into my desk chair.

She got right to the point. "Trey left again last night."

I didn't want her to know that I was already privy to that. If for any reason she slipped and told Trey, then he would probably change tactics. So for now I played along.

"What time?" I asked. Brad's desk phone rang and he snatched it up.

"Around one. He took his boat keys again." She sounded miserable.

"Okay. Look, let me see if I can keep a better eye on him and see where he's going off to."

"You'll do that?"

"Of course."

"What if he's into something...you know—*bad?*"

"Let's cross that bridge when we get there," I said.

"Thanks, Ryan, for helping. It means a lot to have you in my corner on this."

I hung up with Amy at the same time Brad was returning his desk phone to the cradle. "How is she?" he asked.

"Worried. I didn't tell her about last night."

"Yeah, probably best." He slid his fingers over his computer's trackpad and navigated to his email. "So...that was Krugman on the phone. He got a match from our guy last night. He just emailed me what he found. Looks like the guy with the oily hair is a Carlos Vargas." Brad pulled up our internal database and copied over some of the information Krugman had provided. "Here we go," Brad said triumphantly, but it was short-lived, and he started shaking his head. "This is not good. This guy is a really bad apple." I pushed away from my desk and slid my chair around so I was behind him, peering over his shoulder.

My concerns over Trey skyrocketed as I scanned what the screen was displaying: Vargas was a Mexican national wanted for six murders in both Veracruz and Mexico City. At one time he had been a lieutenant in the Zellupa drug cartel before falling out of favor with them and defecting to Honduras three years ago, where he started trafficking in narcotics. There didn't seem to be anything on him after that.

"What's the last thing in his file?"

Brad performed a few different searches across three more federal databases. "That's it. This guy's been a ghost for three years, ever since he got out of Mexico. Nothing but a connection to a drug kingpin in Tegucigalpa."

I sat back and ran my hands through my hair. "What the hell is Trey doing wrapped up with a guy like that?"

"And what's Vargas doing up here?"

The natural conclusion would be that they were running drugs, but it had been three years since Vargas showed up on anyone's radar. He could be into anything by now. "Whatever it is," I said, "the direction is backwards. Trey took something to Vargas last night, not the other way around."

"Yeah. Weird. Any idea who Trey might have access to? I thought he just cut grass and trimmed palm trees, but maybe he has an old friend or a distant relative that's into something and brought him on board."

It was clear enough now why Trey didn't want to open up to me at The Reef the day before, and why Amy said he hadn't been acting like himself. Vargas was a rotten fish— one of the worst, as far as I could tell—and that complicated how I was going to handle this. If I went to Trey and told him we were onto him, then he could warn Vargas, who would then disappear. Then there was the added dynamic that I didn't know what they were doing, or why. Trey might want to keep doing his little side gig, and showing my cards too early could scare him off too.

Brad drummed his fingers on his desk. He looked as worried as I felt. "What are you gonna do?"

"I'm not sure. I need to think about it."

"If you would have told me that Trey was into anything more than scalping tickets for a Marlins game, I wouldn't have believed you. I really did think he was a good kid."

"Yeah." I sighed. "Me too."

I scooted back to my desk and slipped the USB drive into the side port. "Come on. Let's see what's on this thing."

CHAPTER FIFTEEN

"WHAT THE HELL?" Brad squinted at my screen and scratched his chin.

He wasn't the only one underwhelmed by what we were looking at. The small portable drive contained just two files: one Word and one Excel. The latter had nothing but a scattering of numbers across a handful of cells. That was it. No fancy financial spreadsheets put together by some overeager accountant. Not even a secondary tab.

The Word document wasn't much better, albeit it was something. It was just one page with just three names on it.

I clicked around on both documents for the better part of five minutes, trying to find something more substantial, with no luck locating even a revision history. Della had told us that Scahill planned on getting a lot of money for this information when the time was right. He could have easily been lying to her, but then that wouldn't explain the reason why he felt the need to hide the drive in the Coke can.

Brad leaned forward and searched the screen. "What do you think the numbers mean? Coordinates or something?"

"I don't think so." There were dashes between every few numbers. "They don't read like them. Might be banking information."

"Send it over to Spam," Brad said.

"Good call." I crafted an email to Frank Ritter, one of our cyber guys downstairs. Everyone just called him by his nickname. I wasn't sure how the name had stuck, but Krugman told me it had to do with how barstool princesses felt toward him when he tried to use his god-awful pickup lines on them.

If anyone could make sense of this Excel spreadsheet, it would be Spam. I sent the email off and returned to the names.

"Wait a minute..." Brad said. He went back to his desk and returned with a file. He searched through it before plucking out a page. "Here. I knew I recognized that name." He set the page next to my computer. The bold name on the top matched the one on my screen: Ian Foster.

"What's the deal on him?" I asked.

"Foster runs a container refurbishing company near Port-Miami. He sold containers to the Port and to Barker. After Barker's arrest, the DEA questioned Foster, but he came out clean. I haven't found anything else on him."

I ran the other two names, Tina Edwards and Steve Holden, through our database and cross-checked them with other agencies. Nothing came back. Not even a speeding ticket. Not even a listed home address. Just a PO box in South Beach. After a few minutes online, we found an obscure article from a Nassau publication that had done a small feature on the couple, who were apparently dating and traveling around the Caribbean on their yacht. The article was dated nearly four months ago. That was it. Nothing about where they were going next or even the name of their boat.

I looked to Brad. "Their names don't ring a bell for you? Don't recognize them?"

"Nuh-uh. Never heard of them."

"So all Scahill had was a bunch of jumbled numbers and the names of three people. He's dead and two of these names are lost to the wind. It looks like the only thing that came out of that Coke can is a washed up lead in Miami."

Brad offered up a smug smile. "You thinking what I'm thinking?"

"Yeah," I said. "Time to head up to Miami and pay Mr. Foster a visit, warmed over or not."

"What? Dude, that's not what I was thinking at all." He lowered his voice. "Kicking out a little early? The Reef? Beer? And I'm getting to know this new waitress, Lisa—"

"Brad. We're going to Miami."

"Dammit."

CHAPTER SIXTEEN

THE TREADMILL SPED beneath his feet, and he kicked up the pace a few more notches and sprinted out his last quarter mile. Sweat was pouring down his back and his lungs were burning, but he completed his distance goal of three miles.

Trey brought the treadmill's speed down to a walking pace and waited for his heart rate to slow before shutting down the machine and stepping off. He sat down to catch his breath and wiped a towel across his sweaty brow. Tilting his head back, he lifted his water bottle and squeezed some cold water into his mouth. After wiping his lips with the back of his hand, he stood up and started pacing the floor.

His nerve endings were still jittery. He had hoped the exercise would burn off some of the anxiety he was feeling. But it hadn't worked at all. Now he just felt worried *and* tired.

Tossing the towel over his shoulder, Trey headed to the front desk where he asked a fitness instructor for a pen and paper. He stepped to the side and used the counter for a place to write on.

It took him more than fifteen minutes to get his thoughts down, and even then he still wasn't done. Glancing up at the clock on the wall, he realized it was nearly time to head to work. There was grass to cut and hedges to trim.

He walked to the far wall and located his locker. After getting it open, he placed the pen and paper on the shelf.

He would have to finish writing his thoughts down later.

CHAPTER SEVENTEEN

IT WAS JUST after 4:00 PM when we passed into downtown Miami. Car horns and squealing brakes echoed off the windows of the high rises as we headed east on NW 3rd Street.

Titled the "Cruise Capital of the World," PortMiami is the largest passenger port on earth, and one of the largest cargo ports in the U.S. It accounts for nearly three hundred fifty thousand jobs and has an annual economic impact of $43 billion to the Sunshine State. More than ten million tons of cargo and more than one million shipping containers pass through each year.

Tens of millions of dollars of federal funds are spent each year to prevent illegal cargo from coming into the U.S. through this very seaport: black market products, drugs of every type, and even people—poor families from poor Asian countries, looking for a better way of life or kidnapped women intended to be sold to illegal stateside brothels.

Putting downtown behind us, I took Port Boulevard over Biscayne Bay to Dodge Island. After getting through the checkpoint at the port entrance, we navigated past stacks of containers on the south end of the packed island. Everywhere trucks, reach stackers, terminal tractors, and gantry cranes were moving like a coordinated ant colony to reposition containers into their proper places.

Entering the warehouse district, we passed several structures before arriving at a steel-framed building the size of a small airplane hangar. We parked in a space at the front and stepped out into the sunlight just as a reach stacker rolled by.

The vinyl stenciling on the front glass door read *Miami Refurb*. I pulled on the door handle and stepped into a small lobby. The floors were cracked and grimy linoleum tiles; the walls were painted a dark green. A long hallway led to a door at the other end that I presumed opened onto the bay where they worked on the containers. An old lady sat behind an older desk and looked on us with a full measure of indifference.

"Help you?"

"Yes," I said. "My name is Ryan Savage and this is Brad Pierce. We're with the Federal Intelligence Directorate, a division of Homeland Security. We need a few minutes to speak with Mr. Foster."

She didn't seem fazed by the request. "I'll tell him. But I should let you know we just had a new order come in from China. He's pretty swamped right now. I don't know if he'll be able to get free to talk with you."

I decided to wait and see what her boss told her before I let her know that we weren't leaving without speaking to him.

"You can have a seat." She motioned to a couple of chairs behind us, covered in dark green vinyl that was cracked in half a dozen places. The air rushed out of the cushions as they took our weight. The lady picked up the phone and pecked out a four digit number. She spoke softly enough that I couldn't make out what she was saying. Then she placed her palm over the phone's receiver and looked in our direction. "What's this regarding?"

"We'll wait to speak with Mr. Foster about that," I said.

She gave a *hmph* and relayed what I had said into the phone. A few seconds later, she returned it to its cradle. "He said he'll be with you soon."

On an end table next to Brad was an ancient and sunbleached copy of *Ladies' Home Journal.* A younger Julia Roberts was on the cover and a caption promised a recipe for "To Die For Casserole." Brad picked up the magazine and started flipping through it.

"You're kidding, right?"

"What?"

"That's a chick mag. What's wrong with you?"

He lowered the magazine and looked around. "You see anything else to read?"

"No. But reading nothing's better than that."

He shrugged. "I'm a dude. I like casserole. They have articles about casserole. And Julia Roberts." Then he returned his attention to it.

I bounced my heel on the floor and stared down the hallway as the minutes ticked by. I'd never liked waiting. If patience was a virtue, then that was a virtue I was missing and didn't know that I planned to get. I was about to ask the receptionist for an update when a door opened down the hall. A man who looked to be in his mid-forties stepped out. His tapered brown hair was graying at the temples and dark circles sat under shifty eyes. I recognized him from the photo Brad had shown me at the office. Ian Foster gave a brief and nervous glance our way before turning toward the opposite end of the hall and hustling down it.

Normally, I would have just assumed he was taking care of some business before he came to meet with me. But it was those untrained and shifty eyes that gave him away. I stuck Brad in the ribs with an elbow and jutted my chin down the hall. Foster was moving at a healthy pace now and as soon as he burst into the work bay, he started running as the metal door shut behind him.

Brad set the magazine down with a sigh. "It's oregano. *That's* the secret ingredient." We stood up and I tossed him my truck keys. Between us, I was the fastest sprinter. I started down the hall and heard Brad exit the front door while the crusty lady at the front started yelling after me. "Excuse me. Where are you—you can't go back there! Sir!"

I reached the end of the hall, slammed my hand down on the door handle and shouldered the door open. I came out into what amounted to a small airplane hangar. Rusted out containers of every color were stacked along the walls; in the center of the floor, sparks were flying as welders worked to make old containers new. Clear plastic sheets were hung along the back section where the restored containers were given a fresh coat of paint. I looked to the end of the building and saw a sliver of outdoor light disappear as a door at the other end of the building slapped shut. My Glock was still in its holster. So far I hadn't been given a good enough reason to reach for it. But I knew that could change at any second.

I raced toward the door and flung it open, coming out to the back of the buildings. To my left, Biscayne Bay sat below a concrete seawall, on the other side of an old fence. On my right, the building shot a straight line, a single gray wall against which sat a cluster of dumpsters. Foster was straight ahead of me, heading for the nearest turnout. I tore after him and started gaining immediately. He wasn't overweight by any means, but it was clear that he spent all his time behind a desk.

I didn't bother yelling for him to stop. That kind of ridiculousness only happens in the movies—and not good movies. He knew who I represented, and he obviously knew I would have preferred a quiet, professional discussion in his office rather than impromptu tryouts for the 500-meter dash.

He looked over his shoulder and when he saw me approaching at a rapid rate, he hesitated and altered his course. He veered to the right, where an upcoming alley would allow him to route back to the main road.

He shot around the corner and I heard the screech of tires on the pavement, followed by a hollow *thump*. I peeled around the corner to see Foster lying in the alley in front of my truck. Brad was getting out of the driver's seat and came around. We both stared down at the businessman as he writhed on the ground.

Brad looked down at him and shook his head. "What's the big deal, *compadre*? We just want to talk."

We got him to his feet and brushed the gravel off his shirt. He winced when my hand skimmed over his shoulder. Brad snickered. "You know, they say that individuals who don't smoke and don't run from inquiring federal agents live longer than those who do."

"I don't have anything to say to you." Surprisingly, Foster wasn't angry. He was, however, clearly terrified.

"Then why did you run? We just wanted to talk."

He stepped out and twisted in my grip so he could turn and look at me. When he spoke next, his words only confirmed what I saw clearly in his dark eyes. "If I talk to you—if they even think I've talked with you, they'll kill me."

CHAPTER EIGHTEEN

I KEPT my hand firmly on his upper arm and marched him back to his office. As I settled into my chair Brad came in and shut the door behind him. He tossed me my keys and took the chair beside me.

The office was small and unkempt. Boxes of files were stacked along one wall, and I could hardly see Foster's keyboard for all the paperwork strewn across his desk. I didn't know how he could work like that day after day. It would make me a nervous wreck.

I heard the clicking of heels just outside the door, and the secretary opened it and stuck her head in. "Ian, is everything all right?"

"Yes, Nancy. It's fine. You can go back to the front."

She eyed me with a fiery glare that made me slightly worried that she was about to attack me.

"Nancy," Foster snapped. "It's fine. Please."

"Okay..." She stepped out and shut the door. We could hear her mumbling to herself on the way back down the hall.

"She's been with me from the beginning," Foster said. "She's gotten a little edgy since her husband died last year, but she's a good lady."

Brad leaned forward and placed his elbows on his knees. "The DEA came by here a couple months ago. From what I could tell you didn't run from them." He left the question hang.

"That's because since then there's been—well, there's been some developments."

"Oh, I love a good development," Brad said. "Do tell. Let's start with who's going to kill you for talking to us."

Foster let out an exasperated sigh. "That's the thing. I have no idea. I've already told you that I can't tell you anything. And I—I want to call my lawyer."

I leaned back in my chair and crossed my right ankle over my left knee. "You and I both know that only guilty people want to call their lawyers." He started to speak, but I held up a hand. "I'll tell you what. You tell me what I want to know—the truth—and I'll make sure this little container business of yours never gets on the local evening news."

"What? What are you talking about?"

"He's saying," Brad interjected, "that if you don't start freely bubbling over with information, the local news is going to get a tip about this location. Maybe something about you embezzling money from the port, or about your work area back there being a destination hub for trafficked illegals. Lots of attention, that sort of thing."

"You can't—" Foster stopped short. He knew very well what we could do. Foster lowered his voice. "Look, about six months ago Barker came to me to customize some of the containers. I didn't know him before that. He just walked in and told me what he needed."

"And when you say custom..." I knew exactly what he meant, but I wanted to hear it from him.

"A false wall that allowed for a couple of unaccounted feet of space in the back...or a ceiling panel a few inches lower than the top. That kind of thing."

"So you did it for him?"

"Yes—yes, I did it for him, okay? We've been getting more and more underwater over here and the extra cash helped me pay down some creditors so I can keep this place afloat."

"So," Brad said, "since Barker's been dead for a couple of months, what exactly are these new developments you mentioned?"

"As soon as I heard that Barker got arrested for transporting dope on his trucks, I had one of my crews stay on late one night and they disassembled everything we were working on for Barker and got rid of it all. When the DEA came asking questions, there was nothing for them to find. Barker always paid in cash. After he died, I thought we were done. I just—I just wanted things to get back to normal. And they did, until a couple weeks ago. Someone called me from an untraceable number and said that I needed to resume the arrangement I had with Barker. I told him to go to hell and the next morning my dog is dead on the front porch. Someone slit his throat. He bled out on the porch." Foster's face flushed red. "My kid found Skippy like that. My *kid*."

"This guy who called you," I said, "when is he going to pick up the containers?"

"I don't know. I haven't heard from him again. He said to stay on task and he would be back in touch in the next month. That was almost three weeks ago now. But he said if the containers weren't done, I was going to regret it." He huffed. "I already do."

"Be that as it may," Brad said. "When you were doing some work for Barker you still knew what you were doing. You knew those containers were for something illegal."

Foster looked shamefully down at his desk. "I did."

Now we were getting somewhere. "Do you know what that something illegal was, exactly?"

"No. He never told me and I never asked. Our relationship was me strictly filling orders for him based on his specifications." He hesitated, seeming to remember he was speaking with a federal agent. But then he seemed to relent. "I figured it was drugs. It made sense. He ran a trucking company that runs truck cargo up to all areas of the country."

I was just happy we were talking with someone in this investigation that hadn't been killed. *Yet*. Still, we needed more. Foster's admission to his complicity in wrongdoing wasn't going to get Brad and me to the next step. "Have you ever heard the name of an Eric Scahill?

"No. Why?"

"How about a Tina Edwards or Steve Holden?"

The color drained from his face.

"You're a terrific non-verbal communicator." Brad smiled. "Ryan, I think he's heard of Lisa Edwards and Steve Holden before."

"Do tell," I said to Foster.

He swallowed hard and wet his lips. "They—they were private equity investors. They were the ones who directed Barker to come to me and introduced us. But they uh... They're dead."

I exchanged a brief glance with Brad. The bodies were starting to pile up and form a small hill. Barker, Scahill, and now two of the three names that Scahill had on the thumb drive were all dead. Our earlier inquiry into Edwards and Holden at the office hadn't yielded much, but if they were deceased, something would have come back about that. At the very least the Social Security Administration would have it on file, and the state of Florida would have issued a death certificate. Our search query had pulled from both of those databases. I narrowed my eyes on Foster. "How do you know that? There are no records of their deaths."

"Barker told me the day before they raided his business and arrested him."

"And no one has reported them missing in all this time? Forgive me, but Brad here doesn't have a lot of friends, and I promise you that if he had been dead for a couple of months *someone* would start asking questions."

Brad raised a finger. "For the record, I now have one less friend. But he's right, Ian. That doesn't add up for me either."

Foster looked exhausted. All the stress clearly had him on a mental and emotional precipice. "Look, Steve is—was—my old college roommate. He went into the white collar side of this industry and I went with the blue collar. And guess who got the yacht and guess who got a pack of wolves at the door?" He waved off an answer and continued. "Both Steve and Tina were loners. No family and not really any friends. They had each other and they had their money. They invested in micro-cap and struggling companies with their own personal cash. So they had no businesses to get back to and manage. At the same time, I'd known Steve to be the kind of guy to get his hands a little dirty from time to time. Her too, for that matter. When Barker told me they were dead, I figured they got in over their heads and it caught up to them."

"And you don't think you got in over your head?" I asked. "You don't think your dirt is going to catch up to you?"

He just stared at me like a scared animal.

I knew Foster wouldn't go for what I was about to propose, but if I didn't pitch the idea I was going to have him on my conscience for a very long time. "I'm not going to get into specifics, Ian, but I think you're smart enough to know that there's a very good chance that you're on someone's hit list. The guy who ordered more containers or whoever he might be working for. You would qualify for a level of witness protection and—"

"No way." Foster raised his hands and now, oddly enough, he looked more worried than moments before. "No way

I'm going into witness protection. Look, my wife has no idea about the stuff I just told you. She's got the perfect upper-middle class home, country club membership, and the kids are in private school. She's clueless about the downtrending nature of my business financials this last year. If I tell her what I was doing for Barker, she'll leave me and I won't be able to salvage what little we have left between us."

"But you can't work at salvaging a bad marriage if you're dead," Brad said.

"No," Foster said again. "I don't want the kids growing up with their parents split up. I had to do that and it was hell. I'll just"—he swallowed nervously again—"stay the course."

I leaned forward and took a stronger tone. "Ian, I'm not going to give you my business card because I don't carry business cards. But you need to take down my number and make sure you don't misplace it in that pile of trash you call a desk." He dug around and located a pen, then hovered it over a scrap of paper. I recited my phone number. "You call me as soon as you hear from the guy you're building the containers for. At some point, he'll contact you for delivery of the containers you're refitting for him. Correct?"

"Yes."

"So as soon as he does, you're to call me. You'll be scared. You'll wonder if he'll come back and kill your ferret or your wife or your kid if he finds out you're speaking with us. But call me anyway. If you don't, I can make sure you wish you had. Do you understand me?"

He nodded and suddenly looked like he was trying to hold his breath. Then his chest shuddered. The skin on his face became splotchy, and he quickly backed up his desk chair, grabbed an orange hard hat from his desk, and threw up into it.

A bilious stench started to fill the room.

Time to leave.

CHAPTER NINETEEN

IT TOOK us nearly an hour to muscle our way through Miami rush-hour traffic. The honking, the constant stop-and-go, and the exhaust fumes were a clear enough reminder of why I had no desire to live in the city.

"These stupid investigations are always more complex than you think going into them," Brad said. "I don't know why we can't just have two dudes who killed each other over an argument about who gets to plant the bomb. *Bam*. Done. 'Kathleen, I know you just gave us this case three minutes ago, but we solved it.'"

"Maybe if we had Detective Wallace's job," I said.

"Then I want Detective Wallace's job."

"We'll need to dig into Edward's and Holden's financials," I said. "If they were into bad money, then there's a trail there somewhere. And we need to get someone who can locate their yacht."

"I'll check all the Caribbean customs tomorrow," he said. "See if I can find their last port of call. And we need to see about a warrant to tap Foster's cell phone. When he gets that call he's expecting, we need to be able to track it or at the very least listen in."

We finally got out of the city and passed through Homestead. Half an hour later, we passed over Cross Key and came into Key Largo. Home sweet home. I had my cell on a phone clip attached to an air vent. When it rang, I answered it through my truck's Bluetooth. "There's my favorite boss," I said.

"Sucking up to me isn't going to help me forget your wayward ways, Ryan." Still, I heard a smile in Kathleen's voice.

"What's up?"

"The Coast Guard just called the office. They found the skiff that Eric Scahill's murderer got away on earlier today. It was out by Oyster Key caught up in some mangroves."

"Caught up in?"

"Someone poured gasoline over it and set flame to it. They took the outboard off, so no serial numbers, and no decals on the hull. They won't be getting any DNA or prints off of what's left. Another boat probably picked your guy up."

Well, there went that lead. Unless the Sheriff's Office found something in the motel rooms—and I was fairly certain they wouldn't—it looked like Scahill's murderer just got away with it.

Brad spoke with a grin on. "So how do you want us to find a killer with no clues, Kathleen?"

"I think you'll manage. Or maybe not. You've been at the Barker thing for a while and can't find who killed him. Maybe I should fire you both and bring in a couple of agents who know how to actually get things done."

"They *burned* the boat," Brad said. "How do we get around that?"

Ignoring this, she said, "How did Miami go? Are you on your way back yet?" I filled her in on the last couple of hours, how our time at the port had gone, and our conversation with Foster.

"Kathleen?"

"Yes, Brad?"

"We would have found all the evidence, but the old lady at the front set fire to the place and there wasn't anything left to recover."

"Goodnight, guys. I'll see you tomorrow." She disconnected.

"She loves us," Brad said.

"Maybe. I think she loves us more when we close out a case."

"Good point."

A couple of minutes later, my tires crunched into The Reef's parking lot and we went inside. Bob Marley drifting from the speakers and the lively chatter were a welcome reprieve after the day we'd just had. There was something about walking into an island bar that causes all your worries to slip from your shoulders. We bellied up to the bar, and Roscoe came over and took our drink orders: bourbon on the rocks for me and a piña colada for Brad.

The old man studied us and frowned. "You boys look like you've been out on the water fighting with a marlin all day."

"Something like that," Brad said, looking around. "Hey...is uh, Lisa here?"

Roscoe laughed. "Ryan keeps pissing off my female patrons, and you can't stay away from my waitresses."

"Well, start hiring ugly waitresses and I'll start staying away from them."

"Lisa has the day off," Roscoe said. "But I saw the two of you chatting it up last night. Somehow she managed not to miss a beat with the customers. You boys want anything to eat?"

We each put in an order for a burger and found a stool to perch on. Roscoe slid our drinks across the bar top and I saw a glimmer in his eyes. "What?" I said.

"I've decided to take your advice, Ryan, and get a jukebox. It's coming in from South Carolina next week."

I'd been pushing Roscoe to get a jukebox for the better part of a year. You couldn't beat live music, but when the stage was empty, there was nothing like stepping up to a jukebox and selecting your song. "Very cool," I said. "Where are you gonna put it?"

"I was thinking I'd move the trophy display over toward the bathrooms and put the jukebox in its place." Roscoe had more than twenty fishing trophies from tournaments he'd participated in over the years. That man could pull in a fish with more skill and finesse than anyone else I knew. "It's framed in salvaged wood from an old pirate ship."

Brad took a generous gulp of his piña colada and winced against the cold as he swallowed. "Will it have *'Achy Breaky Heart'* on it?"

"Absolutely," Roscoe said.

I groaned.

"If it's any consolation," Roscoe said, "I'll make sure it has Van Morrison and Pearl Jam."

"Now you're talking."

CHAPTER TWENTY

I woke the next morning to the sound of a fish splashing in the water and the sky tinged with the blue glow of early dawn. I stretched, yawned, and then turned back over and closed my eyes. I typically roll out of bed pretty easily. But the nature of my time spent in Guatemala hadn't allowed me much of an opportunity to sleep while I was there. And I'd been going nonstop ever since I got back.

I focused on the sound of my breathing, hoping it would lull me back to sleep, but another fish splashed a few slips down, and I heard the gentle whoosh of a pelican's wings as it coasted by my half-open window. Across the dock, a motor yacht started up and a steady hum growled across the marina.

I wasn't going back to sleep.

Reluctantly, I rolled out of bed and knocked out my exercise routine before making a cup of coffee and heading up to the top deck. The horizon was tinted a bright yellow and orange and a gentle breeze blew over me. It was moments like these that made you thankful for what you had. I'd lost a lot these past couple of years, but I still knew I was lucky to be living in the Keys. It was a gift I planned to never take for granted.

"Morning, Ryan!"

I stood up and turned to see Rich Wilson strolling down the dock, his tiny Yorkshire terrier alongside him. He and his wife lived on a cruising catamaran a few slips down from me. That dog got him up every morning well before any of us other liveaboards would ever consider waking up. Rich was hefty, had silky white hair and a gentle, booming voice. The sunsets, the water, the fish, and the music were just some of the things that made this place a paradise. But it was also the people. Rich had spent nearly thirty years as a New York police officer before he and Edith bought the catamaran last year. They had come to feel a lot like what I figured an aunt and uncle must be like. My parents were in France when they got in their fatal car crash. I was only five. They were in Europe celebrating their ten year wedding anniversary. And by some sort of cosmic joke, they never made it back, leaving me with very few memories of the times I had with them. Their only child, I went to live with my grandmother. She was all I had; I never did have cousins or extended relatives, no family reunions or an uncle to take me camping. Since I moved here, Rich and Edith had become like the family I never had. They tied up here in Key Largo more than a year ago. I knew they would leave for different waters one of these days, and I would be sorry when they did.

"Hi, Rich. Beautiful morning."

"The best. Edith was just mentioning last night that we haven't seen you around much lately."

"I was out of the country for a couple of weeks. I got back two days ago."

"Out of the country, huh? Which one did you visit?"

"Guatemala."

His face pinched and he looked up at me. "Guatemala? We just heard on yesterday's news that the mansion of some big name counterfeiter burned down. Or was set fire to. Were you close to all that?" Rich didn't know what I did—not exactly. That decision on my part was mostly because Edith was a worry-wart. If she knew that much of my time was spent chasing down the worst of the worst, I'd never hear the end of her concerns.

I kept it so most everyone knew simply that I worked for the government. When pressed, I always kept my answers general, stating I worked to ensure that federal protocols were followed by appointed liaisons at the state level. That usually got their eyes to glaze over pretty well, and any further inquiry into my profession was dropped. I didn't work for the CIA or the NSA, and the FID wasn't a secret agency, so I didn't have to keep my employer off anyone's radar. But connections were tight down here, and all I needed was for the wrong people to catch wind of what I did. If that happened, I could all but say goodbye to my anonymity as an investigator. Local detectives with the Sheriff's Office might not worry about the public knowing what they did, but Brad and I certainly did.

"No," I replied. "I was back before that. Looks like a big fiasco, though."

"You can say that again! I heard there were tens of millions of counterfeits in that house. Or there were before they torched it." He shook his head. "You know, Ryan. I saw a lot of stuff during my time with the NYPD. Stuff that would make your head spin if I told you. But I never do get used to stories of brazen crimes. Some people never will stop doing the wrong thing to get what they want. It's almost like they were born to it—No, Sunny!" Sunny, his dog, looked like he was about to hop onto the transom and board an empty fishing boat. Sunny barked at his owner and then came and sat at Rich's feet. "Good dog. Well, Ryan. I'd better get back. Edith wants us to drive up to Fort Lauderdale today so she can spend some time with her sister."

We said goodbye and I returned to my stateroom. I had just peeled off my shirt and shorts when my phone rang. It was Brad.

"Hey, you at the office yet?"

"Nope," I said.

"Okay, well I couldn't sleep last night, so I stayed up trying to make sense of everything Foster told us."

"Thanks for calling to tell me that."

"I need you to meet me at my place. Twenty minutes."

"I'm about to get in the shower."

"Okay, fine. Twenty-two minutes. Then we're going to Cudjoe Key."

Cudjoe Key was an hour and a half from Key Largo, half an hour east of Key West. I was there last month and enjoyed a weekend of scuba diving. "What's down there?" I asked.

"I'll tell you when you get here. Hurry up. And don't forget to wash behind your ears."

CHAPTER TWENTY-ONE

I MADE sure to take my time in the shower and showed up to Brad's more than a half an hour later. He was already in his Jeep with the engine running. I parked beside it and then switched vehicles. As I opened the door to the Jeep, Brad said, "You're late. What'd you do, let your conditioner set?"

"I don't like being rushed in the mornings. You know that." Brad checked his rearview, backed up, and then shot down the main road through his small neighborhood. A minute later we were on the Overseas Highway speeding west. "So why the rush?"

He grabbed his tumbler from the cup holder, took a sip, and then returned it to its spot. "Okay. So I'm lying in bed last night just watching my ceiling blades go 'round, and I got to thinking about Barker's trucking company. Between the FBI, the DEA, and us, we looked at everybody who worked for him. His drivers, suppliers, office staff...all of them. But that was two months ago now, and I got to figuring that they've moved on and all gotten new jobs somewhere. So if any of them were knowingly involved in moving drugs for a supplier when they were with Barker, then what if the supplier kept them on their payroll in some other capacity?"

"And?"

"And so I got up and powered up my laptop. Two people ended up catching my interest. The first was a young guy from Mexico who had been in the U.S. on a worker's visa. But he's back in Mexico City now. But this other guy, he's worth taking a second look at. The DEA took a long look at him but never found a reason to arrest him. They couldn't come up with any proof that he was knowingly moving dope."

"So what's he doing now?"

"Running a charter in the Lower Keys."

"Why's that a red flag? That's what people do down here."

"Because it doesn't add up with this guy—Gregory Sanchez, but he goes by Grecko. He did some time a while back for selling unregistered firearms on the black market. Got out of prison three years ago and got his CDL license, started driving trucks. Soon after his parole was over, he went to work for Barker driving trucks." Brad paused long enough to take another sip of his coffee. "But a fishing charter doesn't seem to fit. He was a Miami gangster, then a truck driver. I don't see where he ever spent much time on the water."

"Where's he dock at?"

Brad gave a knowing smile. "It's Cudjoe Key. Wanna take a guess?"

"Dale's place?"

"Yep. The Blue Tortoise. I called Dale earlier and asked him what he knows about Grecko. He said Grecko goes out just once a week, same time every week, like clockwork, and is back within a few hours. And the weird thing is, he goes out by himself. No guests, no friends, and no paying customers. When he comes back in he's got a couple of coolers full of fish."

"Once a week," I said. "That's a little strange for someone claiming to run a fishing charter."

"He doesn't have another job either."

We passed up Knights Key and rode across to the Seven Mile Bridge, the iconic stretch of road that connects the Middle Key to the Lower Keys. On either side of us, there was nothing but water as far as the eye could see. My kind of place.

After passing up Big Pine and Summerland Keys, we arrived on Cudjoe where Brad left the highway and, after making a few turns, parked in front of the Blue Tortoise Marina. The narrow building was painted a navy blue and a couple of window units hummed loudly as they worked nonstop to keep the inside cool. There were about thirty slips in the little marina, half of them empty at this time of the morning.

We stepped out of the Jeep and as we walked toward the building, I made sure my shirt was draped over my sidearm. A bell rang above the door signaling our entrance. Dale was behind the counter spooling a reel and we worked our way toward him, navigating display stands filled with hooks, lures, and all manner of fish attractants. Along the wall opposite the counter were several refrigerators filled with live bait and bait tanks teeming with live shrimp and minnows.

"Well, look at what the buzzards left behind." Dale wasn't just anybody; he was Roscoe's brother. They were twins, and up until a few months ago, it was nearly impossible to tell the two of them apart, even for those of us who know them well. The defining event came when Dale shaved off his mustache. Before that, about the only way to tell them apart was when they spoke. Roscoe had a deep, resonating voice, Dale a softer, throatier one. He came out from around the counter.

"Good to see you two." We shook hands and he returned to his wooden stool behind the counter and continued working the new line onto the reel. "You boys down here for that Grecko fella?"

"Yes, sir," Brad said. "Has he come back in yet?"

"No..." Dale turned and looked up at the clock on the wall; its short and long hands were tiny fishing poles. "He usually heads out at around four in the morning and is back by nine thirty or ten. So I would expect him back any time now. You think he's up to no good?"

"Maybe," I said. "He really only goes out once a week?"

"Yeah. Which wouldn't be so strange except that he's set up as a charter operation. I've just never seen him use the boat for anyone but himself. That, and he brings back a whole mess of fish for one person to have caught in such a short amount of time. Maybe he trades with someone." Dale shook his head and his brows furrowed. "I hope he's not into anything he shouldn't be. I kinda like the guy. He's always friendly and pays his slip rent on time."

We shot the breeze for half an hour and hung back when a customer came through. When we were alone again, I returned to the counter. "I noticed you painted the exterior since we were here last," I said. "Why the change?" The building used to be a bright canary yellow.

"I named the place *The Blue Tortoise* when I opened it years ago. I figured it was time to have something blue around here besides the bait tanks." Dale looked over and squinted out the window. "Here he comes now." Brad and I stepped to the side door near the register and watched through the glass as an old bluewater battlewagon—a sportfishing boat —idled past the markers and made its way to the marina. "It's always just him on board," Dale said and looked to us. "I usually go help him tie off. That still okay to do?"

"Sure," I said. "Just don't act any differently than you usually do."

Dale nodded his understanding, and we stepped back so he could open the door. We watched as he moved down the dock and stopped at a slip near the end. The boat's fenders were already out and the captain slowly backed into the slip. Dale grabbed a line and tied off on a cleat before hurrying around to starboard and securing the boat from that side. At the end of the dock was a small shed next to the gas pump. Dale disappeared into the shed and returned a moment later pushing a dolly in front of him.

The man we took to be Grecko appeared out of the cockpit. He had to be one of the largest men I'd ever seen. Beside me, Brad let out a low whistle. "He makes a sumo wrestler look small."

Grecko had dark ruddy skin that testified to Latino descent. His round face matched the shape of his body and he worked his way across the deck to the stern, where he picked up an ice chest and heaved it over the gunwale to Dale. Dale took it and dropped it onto the dolly. They repeated the process for one more ice chest. After exchanging a few words, Dale made his way back to the shop. After stepping off the boat Grecko tipped back the dolly and headed down the dock.

When Dale came back in, he looked at us and shrugged. "That's what we do every Thursday morning like clockwork. Like I said, never had any problems with him."

Keeping my eye on Grecko, I said, "Let's go see what's in those coolers." Brad followed me out and we waited for the big man to turn and start heading toward the parking lot before approaching him from behind.

"Excuse me, sir. You have a minute?"

Grecko stopped and turned around. He gave the two of us a suspicious glare but said nothing. I introduced Brad and myself, and when Grecko heard the combined terms of FID and Homeland, he looked like he was thinking about running. But the intensity in his face waned as he seemed to understand that he would probably have a difficult time outrunning me. "What do you want?"

"You're Gregory Sanchez?"

"Yes."

Smiling cordially at him, I said, "Can you tell us where you've been the last few hours?"

"I was out fishing on Pourtalès Terrace. Something wrong?"

Pourtalès Terrace is an underwater steep-walled depression halfway between the Keys and the Bahamas. It was feasible that he could get out there within an hour.

"And you have fish in the ice chests?"

"Yes. Pompano."

"Would you mind if we take a look?"

"I'm sorta in a hurry. The fish aren't on ice and I need to get them to my buyer."

"Understood," I said. "It will literally take about thirty seconds. That okay?"

The large man hesitated. Each time he took in a breath it was a labored, wheezing effort.

He looked nervously at the dolly and then back to us. "No. Like I said, I just have my catch in here. Do you have a warrant or something? I haven't done anything."

"Look, Mr. Sanchez—I hear that people call you Grecko. You okay if I call you Grecko?"

"Sure." He was looking more nervous by the minute. Sweat glistened off his forehead and over the last minute, his pupils had gotten wider. He was clearly uncomfortable.

"Grecko, here's the thing. I can either find a good reason to bring you in for questioning, in which case we'll still look inside your ice chests and then we'll also search your boat, your vehicle, and probably your house, too, or we can just take a peek at your catch right now."

Jutting his thumb toward me, Brad said, "He's got a thing for pompano. All he wants to do is see your fish. Then we'll be out of your way."

Grecko pursed his lips hard, and I couldn't tell if he was having a heart attack or just trying to think of what to say next. Finally, he directed an open palm toward the dolly's contents. "Go ahead."

Brad grabbed the top ice chest and set it at his feet. "Are you armed?" he asked Grecko. "Any weapons on you?" The last thing we wanted was to find something in among the fish and have him reach for a gun in the back band of his shorts.

"No," he answered. He could be lying, but at least now he knew where our own thoughts were.

"Great." I stood back and kept an eye on Grecko as Brad lifted the lid and looked inside. He nodded. "Impressive," he said. "That's a good catch. Although some of these are way under your eleven-inch minimum size limit, and you're obviously way over your six per harvester limit."

"I didn't—"

"It's okay," I interrupted. "We're not Fish and Wildlife."

Grecko seemed to relax at that but quickly tensed as he watched Brad shoot a hand inside the chest and work it in past the fish. "Slimy," he muttered and then stopped short and looked over at me. "And not slimy."

"Do you have anything else in there besides fish?" I asked Grecko.

"Uh, just an old radio transmitter that I wrapped up."

Brad brought his hand out and shook it, then he grabbed the side of the ice chest and heaved it over. Dead pompano poured out and some slithered off across the dock. When Brad pulled the ice chest away from the fish, Grecko shifted nervously on his feet. The corner of a large black package protruded from the silvery pile.

Smiling at him, I said, "That's your radio transmitter?" He looked like he was going to say something but then changed his mind and stayed silent.

Brad and I changed positions as I brought out my switchblade and exposed the blade with a flick of my wrist. Brad kept watch on Grecko as I squatted down and worked the tip of my blade beneath the plastic, which was wrapped tightly around contents that were shaped together like a large stack of books.

"Careful," Brad told me, "make sure not to cut the *radio*."

After getting the blade inserted properly, I slid it down the edge. The packaging reminded me of bricks of cocaine. The last thing I wanted to do was slice into it at the wrong angle and get the white powder all over me and the dock. Finally, I'd sliced through enough of the wrapping where I could pry it back and see inside. I closed my knife and pulled back the dark plastic. I leaned over and blinked, then looked to Brad, who was grinning out of the side of his mouth. "Does that radio transmitter happen to look like drugs?" he asked.

"No," I said. "It actually doesn't."

"What?" He craned his neck to get a better view. "Then what is it?"

It was money.

Lots and lots of money.

CHAPTER TWENTY-TWO

GRECKO'S EYES went to his feet, and he said nothing and offered no resistance as Brad clicked a pair of handcuffs around his ample wrists. I dumped the second ice chest and found the same thing: a wrapped package of tightly packed hundred dollar bills. A half-inch stack of Ben Franklins is worth ten thousand dollars. I had two packages over one foot high and two feet wide. Doing some quick mental math, I figured I was looking at nearly four million dollars. If Grecko was bringing in this same amount of money once a week, that means he was moving upwards of fifteen million dollars a month.

I didn't know much about Grecko, but I didn't peg him for the kind of guy who could make this kind of money. This wasn't his show—he was a mule, plain and simple.

Fortunately, I had a knack for getting mules to talk.

Dale came out looking a little uncertainly at the man standing on his dock in handcuffs. "Ryan, Brad? Can I...help you two with anything?"

"You can get these fish back in the ice chests," I said. "Make sure you get some gloves on first and leave them behind your counter. Someone will be by for them in a couple hours."

I got on the phone with the FID lab in Key Largo. They would need to come analyze the ice chests for fingerprints, document the evidence, and search Grecko's boat. For reasons of my own, I withheld mentioning Grecko's name during the short conversation. I wasn't going to wait two hours for them to show up, so I told Dale to watch the boat and to call me if he saw anyone snooping around it before our team arrived. Then I borrowed some tape from Dale, wrapped the money up, and transferred it to Brad's Jeep.

We escorted Grecko to the Jeep's front passenger seat and when he sat down, there was a noticeable lean to the right. Brad started griping as we pulled out of the marina. "If I have to get the suspension fixed on this baby because of you I'm taking some of that money in the back to do it."

We drove thirty miles east to Marathon and, after explaining our situation to a deputy at the Sheriff's Office, they let us borrow an interrogation room. We put the money into evidence and then stood around and shot the breeze with the guys and gals from local law enforcement for a while. I wanted Grecko to have some time to sit, think, and possibly work up a nervous sweat before going into the small room and laying his options before him. After whittling half an hour away and ingesting a couple of leftover doughnuts, I spent some time on a borrowed computer reviewing Grecko's file. Brad eventually appeared behind me, standing over my shoulder while working on another doughnut.

"Grecko doesn't seem like the snitching type," I said, "When he went to prison for dealing arms, the arresting detective gave him a chance to rat out his crew for a reduced sentence. He took the full time and didn't say a peep."

"He'll talk," Brad said. His tone was definitive, like he already knew the outcome.

"He didn't snitch then. Why would he now?"

Swallowing the last of his doughnut, he said, "Because I have a secret weapon. Come on. Let's go."

I logged off and walked down the narrow hallway to the metal door at the end. I nodded to the camera in the corner and when the lock buzzed, I pushed it open and stepped inside to have a talk with the best paid charter captain in the Keys.

* * *

I SAT down across from Grecko and he stared angrily at me. "All right," I said. "I've got a proposal I want to put in front of you. I'm sure you're considering asking for a lawyer. And that's your right. However, as soon as you request a lawyer, since this isn't Gitmo, I'll have to oblige you. But once you do that, I'll be unable to make you a deal of my own."

Brad leaned in and whispered across the table. "If he's willing to make you a deal, then that means he's in a decent mood. Which is good for you. I've seen Agent Savage in a bad mood and, well,"—he shook his head —"it's not awesome."

The big man shifted his posture, which received a groan and a creak from the chair. "Earlier this year you drove a truck for Jim Barker," I said. "Are you aware that he was killed two months ago?"

"Yeah. I heard."

"Any ideas why?"

"Nope. People get killed. It happens. Why would I know anything about that?"

"But you know why his business was raided by the DEA."

"The rumor was that he was using some of his trucks to move dope across interstate lines."

"And you knew nothing about that at the time?" Brad asked.

"No. The DEA already questioned me about that. They believed me."

I knew there was a big difference between believing someone and simply lacking the evidence to arrest them. "Okay, fine," I said. "You knew nothing about that. But after Barker's business was suspended, you left, bought a boat, and suddenly start catching fish and money. So now instead of moving drugs for Barker, you're moving the drug dealer's profits into the country?" I stared at him unblinking.

Grecko shrugged. "I got nothing to say."

Finally, Brad said, "Look, you're looking at twenty-to-thirty for that extra bit of cargo you had among your fish. All we want to know is where you got it from."

He shook his head and looked away. "I can't tell you that."

"Okay." Brad slipped a hand into a pocket and withdrew a slip of paper. Unfolding it, he set it face up on the table and slid it across. When Grecko looked down on the picture of his four-year-old daughter, his lip curled and a fresh fire burned in his eyes.

"What are you doing?" he asked through gritted teeth. "You threatening my family?"

Brad huffed. "No, you dimwit. I'm not threatening your family. I'm giving you a chance to reduce your time behind bars so you can actually be a part of her life. Or would you rather be locked up for the next two decades only to get a call from your wife one day—or probably your ex-wife by then—and listen as she tells you that your teenage daughter is pregnant? Right now you're looking at at least twenty years, Grecko. You give us something that helps me shut down the people you're working with and I can probably get you out in five. Maybe less."

Grecko studied his sausage fingers for a long while. Finally he said, "I want your offer in writing."

I shook my head. "Sorry, but you're sitting in the 'no negotiation' chair. You're going to have to take my word. If you can't, fine. You're not our only lead and I'm not waiting for a lawyer or paperwork to slow down my investigation. Talk now, or you'll get transferred up to Miami and won't see me again until I testify against you at your trial."

"This is a one-time offer," Brad said. "We walk out that door over there and you can say goodbye to Krispy Kreme and Chef Boyardee for a very, very long time."

Grecko looked away and worked his jaw like he was thinking, like he was considering letting the proverbial cat out of the bag. "You can get me reduced time?" he asked uncertainly.

"Yes," I said. "You give us something that directly leads to us shutting your operation down, and I can guarantee you that."

When Grecko finally sighed and his shoulders slumped, I knew we had him. "Okay," he said slowly. "Fine."

Not wasting any more time, I jumped right in. "Where do you take the money?"

"To a storage unit up in Homestead. One of those climate-controlled ones. I don't know who comes and gets it. A few weeks ago, I couldn't find my wallet so I finally went back and checked the unit. It had fallen out on the floor in there. That was a couple of days after I dropped off the money and that particular batch was still there. It's always gone by the next week when I drop off a new batch."

I had him recite the address and keypad combination. He said the key to the unit's lock was on the keychain we had already relieved him of. He went on: "You need to know that the money...it's not from the cartels. It's not even drug money."

"Then what it is from?" I asked.

"It's not 'from' anything. It's what it is. Money."

"Obviously it's money," I said. "What product was sold in order to acquire it?"

He looked at both of us with a measure of astonishment. "What kind of investigators are you two, anyway?"

"Handsome ones," Brad retorted. "What else?"

"You're not getting it," Grecko said. "The money I bring in isn't the profits from some kind of black market commerce."

"So...then what is it?"

"It's counterfeit. From Guatemala."

CHAPTER TWENTY-THREE

I FELT a rush of adrenaline course through my body as I listened to Grecko's words. I saw Brad shoot me a glance out of the corner of my eye, but I didn't turn to look at him. "Guatemala?" I said. "You mean to tell me that you've been moving money for Rico Gallardo?"

Grecko seemed pleased that I knew the name. "Gallardo," he said. "Yes. But not for him directly. His people create the money, and I'm just one of the ways they bring it into the country."

"And Barker had you moving Gallardo's money?"

"Yes."

Finally, we were getting somewhere.

Grecko continued. "When Barker got arrested, they came to me directly and offered me a chance to keep working for them. They got me the boat and pay me pretty well."

I had killed Rico Gallardo, but that didn't mean that the money he counterfeited vanished into the underworld with him. The CIA and the Secret Service had yet to identify or shut down all the networks used to move his money around. Then there were the truckloads of fake cash that had been stolen from his mansion. There were still plenty of people hanging around who weren't about to get cheated out of their share of the pie. "And who is 'they'?" I asked.

"All I've ever worked with is one person. We meet once a week for me to pick up the product. He's the same guy who got Barker to work with him."

Brad spread his hands. "And does this guy have a name?"

"I don't know his first name. They try to keep everything fenced off so no one can rat out someone else. But his last name is Vargas."

I looked to Brad. He appeared as astonished as I was. There were thousands of men with that last name, but I didn't believe in coincidences. No good law enforcement officer does.

Grecko studied us. "You know him?"

I used my phone to quickly log into the FID servers via a secure VPN. After locating Carlos Vargas's photo, I turned the screen around toward Grecko. His expression told me everything I needed to know. I put my phone down. "Where do you meet him when you take the boat out every Thursday?"

"Today was supposed to be my last regular meeting with Vargas. We would typically meet in a spot off of Pourtalès Terrace. But I was getting a promotion of sorts. Today he gave me a Bahamian passport; I was going to start working out of the Bahamas."

Grecko didn't have a fake passport on his person when we arrested him. "The passport. It's still on the boat?"

"Yeah," he said. "In a compartment next to the helm."

The door to the interrogation room opened, and a deputy popped his head in. "Hey, guys, someone from your agency is here to pick up the money you brought in."

Brad pushed back his chair and stood up. He tugged up on the waistband of his jeans. "I'll take care of it," he said.

Brad was stepping out to ensure the transfer of possession was made without incident. He would also inform our team to slip a tracker into the packaging before they put it into the storage unit. After that, it would just be a matter of tracking where it traveled inland. After he was gone, I continued with my line of questioning.

"They're going to start running the money through a new channel," Grecko said. "They were putting me out there for the next couple of months to make sure everything goes as planned." He seemed pleased at his apparent promotion.

"And where is this place?"

"Vargas showed me on a map. I'm supposed to take the boat out there five days from this morning." Greco shrugged. "It's south of Andros Town, but I can't tell you without a map."

I stood up, left the room, and walked down the hall to the offices. On a center wall, behind a row of desks, was a large map showing the bottom third of Florida, the Keys, Cuba, and the Bahamas. The map was secured to the wall by means of half a dozen push pins. As soon as I started plucking them out of the sheetrock, a detective objected from behind me.

"Hey, what are you doing? You can't do that!"

I swiveled in his direction. Half the map was reaching limply toward the floor now. "I'm sorry. Are you using it right now?"

"Well, no. But you can't just—"

"Then shut your piehole and let me do my job." I could feel his glare on the back of my head.

I had the entire map off the wall within a few seconds and as I walked back down the hall, it opened like a sail in the breeze, scraping against the sides of the wall. It probably would have been better had I taken the time to roll it up, but I was more concerned with finding out where Grecko's next meeting was supposed to be than about ripping a map in a couple of places.

I reentered the interrogation room and spread the large sheet of paper across the table, the surface of which was much smaller than the map, which hung loosely over the sides and drooped toward the floor. It took me a little while to get the Bahamas centered in front of Grecko.

"All right," I said. "Where are you meeting Vargas?"

He squinted down like he was in need of a pair of eyeglasses and lowered his face toward the map. After half a minute of searching, he sat back up and his handcuffs rattled as he lifted his hands and used a finger to point at a spot. "Right here." Then he removed his finger so I could get a better look.

The Bahamas is an archipelago composed of more than seven hundred islands. Andros Island was the largest of these islands, and at 2,300 square miles had more land mass than all the others combined. Other than North Cat Cay and South Bimini, it was also the nearest Bahamian island to the United States. The more popular Nassau lay on New Providence Island, twenty-five miles to the east.

Grecko had pointed to a cove on the east side of Andros Island, just below the southernmost point of the Queen's Highway. "It's there," he said. "Vargas said there's a small shack at that spot with plumbing and electricity. That's where I'll be staying and where some of the transfers will take place. It's going to be a small hub of sorts hidden away from the coast."

The door opened again and Brad stepped in. He was carrying a Styrofoam plate with three doughnuts on it. He looked pleased with himself.

"You've got to be kidding me," I said.

"Hey," he chided. "These aren't for you." He stepped over to Grecko and extended the plate. "A peace offering," he said and then stifled a yawn. "But a fair warning, they're guaranteed to put you in a coma for the rest of the afternoon."

Grecko stared at the plate's contents for a moment and then picked up a doughnut. He put it in his mouth. I waited for him to finish chewing before continuing. "Is Vargas the boss?"

"No," he said. "Not *the* boss. I report to him, though. He's high up. But no one knows who the big man is. Especially now that Gallardo is dead. Some guy in South America to be sure. But I don't have any idea who's behind getting everything into the U.S."

"Do you have any plans with anyone from the organization over the next several days? Anyone that will notice you're not around?"

"No. I'm not scheduled to take the boat to Andros Island for another five days. I just stay at home with my family in between. I can make a call to my wife if you need me to."

I liked that he was suddenly being so helpful. The threat of not seeing his little girl grow up was clearly a strong motivator.

"I'm going to make sure no one from my office logs your arrest record," I said. "I didn't tell anyone here at this office or mine who you are. I'll have someone from my unit come and transfer you to a private Homeland holding site. Basically it's a place where we can retain you without formally entering you into the system. I don't want Vargas and his guys to catch wind that we have you."

"Yeah," Grecko said. "If he did know he'd change all his plans for sure."

I grabbed the map and started rolling it up. By the time I got done it looked like a crinkled roll of newspapers.

"We'll be in touch," I told him. "If your info doesn't pan out, you won't see daylight for a very long time. If it does, we'll be in your corner."

"It'll pan out," he said confidently. "I told you what I know."

"Either way," Brad said, "If you want to be in your daughter's life ten years from now, you might want to start going easy on the tamales, *Amigo*."

Grecko raised his hands and then lifted his middle finger. I chuckled as Brad and I left the room.

The door had hardly shut when Brad spoke up. "Dude. That Vargas guy is bringing in Gallardo's money and Trey's working with him! You need to have another chat with that boy, and pronto. There's no way he knows what he's gotten into."

Brad was right. I'd known enough people in my life who seemed destined for trouble. Like they enjoyed stepping outside the law and living in the darkness. But Trey wasn't one of those people. I knew that, deep down, he was a good kid. How he'd gotten mixed up with Vargas, and what he was doing for him was still anyone's guess.

"Wanna take a day trip to the Bahamas tomorrow?" Brad asked. "I say we go have a look see over at Andros Island."

"Yeah," I said. "And why don't you put in a call to the U.S. Marshals Service. With all these interrelated murders, we need to see about getting his family some protection until we figure all this out."

"Will do."

We entered the main room again and I unraveled the map. Brad helped me pin it back to the wall and when we were done, we stepped back and took a look at it. I grimaced and Brad stuffed his hands in his pockets and slowly exited the room. The map looked like a crinkled sheet of aluminum foil. There was no way it was getting flat again. Feeling a little bad about that, I quickly followed Brad back through the lobby where we said goodbye to a couple of deputies before making our way back outside.

"Hey," I said, "Are you still going out with Lisa tonight?"

"I was. But she had to cancel. She texted a couple hours ago and said her sister got in a car wreck in Fort Lauderdale. She had to go up there and check on her."

"Or maybe she just smartened up and found a creative way to bail on you."

"Whatever."

CHAPTER TWENTY-FOUR

BRAD DROPPED me back off at my place and went back to the office to update Kathleen on our morning. I decided to slip over to The Reef to grab lunch and spend some time mentally working through the events of the morning. I ordered three fish tacos and waited at the bar until my order came out of the kitchen. I didn't drink when on duty, so I was enjoying a sweet tea instead. The Keys weren't well-known for offering sweet tea, and it was one of the things that attracted me to The Reef when I moved down here two years ago. My wife had been born and raised in Atlanta, and after more than nine years of marriage, she got me hooked on the stuff.

I kept my focus on the TV above the bar where ESPN was showing highlights of the past weekend's football games. After a while Roscoe came out with a basket filled with my food.

"Here you are, good sir. I added in a new sauce at the bottom. Has a bit more of a kick than usual. Let me know what you think."

"Certainly will. Where's Amy? She off today?"

"She went home for a few. Should be back after a little while." He excused himself and returned to the kitchen to start cleaning up after the lunch rush. I slid off my stool, went out on the back deck, and chose a table that let me take in the view of the dock and marina as I ate. In the distance a fishing boat was speeding toward the open ocean up on plane, leaving a trail of white foam on the water's surface behind it.

I thought about Trey as I ate, wondering how in the hell he'd ended up working with Vargas, and what had compelled him to do so. It didn't fit what we all knew about him. That kid was in way over his head—a minnow swimming with the sharks. I decided I would invite him out onto my Whaler when he got off work. Maybe getting him out on the water with a fishing pole and a couple of beers might get him to loosen his tongue.

I had just popped my last hush puppy in my mouth when I felt a firm hand clap me on the back and friendly voice that didn't fit into the context.

"There he is! I was hoping I might find you over here."

I started to turn and stopped chewing when I looked up and saw Special Agent Bud Cole step around me.

"Bud," I said and stood up. I went to shake his hand but stopped short. His right arm was in a sling and his face was full of tiny red nicks where fresh scabs had formed. Still, he had a smile on his face and his bald head glowed like a medallion in the afternoon sun. "What are you doing here? I tried calling you as soon as I heard the news."

He waved off my stunted handshake with his good hand, then reached into his pocket and brought out a cell phone. "Just got this a couple hours ago. I don't think all the voice-mails and texts have changed over yet. Same number though."

I started to sit back down and extended my hand toward the chair across from me. He sat and then scooted his chair in so he was under the shade of the table umbrella. "I got back from Guatemala yesterday afternoon. Spent a couple hours at the hospital and after a multi-hour debrief at my office, they told me to take the rest of the week off. If they need me for anything they'll call or have me come in."

"What are you doing in Key Largo?"

"With a few days off, I thought I'd go see a cousin down in Marathon. I remembered you talking about this place and was hoping you might be here. If not I was going to stop by your office on my way down US-1. I would have just called you, but my contacts haven't updated yet."

"Bud, what the hell happened down there?" It looked like my question pained him. I knew the events were still fresh in his mind.

"It was a first class screw up, that's what. We should have been ready for something like that. Between us and the CIA, we had ten people guarding the mansion's perimeter at any given time. But that was no match for what came at us." He shook his head, frustrated. "They had RPGs, machine guns, and there must have been five times as many men as us."

"Do we know who it was?"

"No, not yet. And there were another half a dozen inside working around the clock to catalog the money. Robbie Stanton was killed."

"I heard. That sucks."

"And the CIA lost four men."

"Four?"

"The news isn't reporting it because the CIA is technically not there."

Bud looked exhausted, if not beat down and defeated. After a silent, internal debate, I decided not to tell him about my morning with Grecko. I was going to find out who was behind the assault on him and his team and present them to him on a silver platter.

"You want a beer?" I asked.

He raised his hand. "No. Waiting until I get to Marathon. But you'd better believe I'm getting hammered tonight."

We talked for another twenty minutes, mostly speculating on what went wrong in Guatemala. Bud finally stood up to leave.

"I'll be back at the Miami office next week," he said. "Stop by sometime. I know the rest of the team would love to see you. They thought you were a first-class guy to work with."

"Thanks, Bud. I'll do that."

After he left I returned to staring at the water. I could feel a hot anger growing inside me by the minute. I had half a mind to call Brad and tell him we were going to the Bahamas right now, but I knew it was too late in the day to account for enough daylight should we find ourselves in need of more of it. My thoughts returned to the pieces Grecko gave us this morning. So far we knew that Carlos Vargas was mid-level management for an operation that was bringing in what was left of Gallardo's counterfeit money. A wealthy couple with a yacht had been murdered, but no one seemed to know just where their boat was or where they were last seen. And Trey was somehow involved.

We were getting close.

The money was currently on the way to the storage unit, and the trackers would let us know where it ended up. And the following morning, Brad and I would head over to Andros Island to see what kind of new setup Grecko had planned on becoming a part of. I pulled out my phone to send Trey a text about the possibility of fishing tonight when a loud, anxious murmur started up around the bar. I went inside to see Roscoe leaning against it with his hands spread out. He looked like he was trying to keep his balance and his face was a much brighter red than was typical. Like candy apple red. I shot around the bar and put a hand on his large shoulder. "Hey, you okay?" He silently nodded his head, but I wasn't convinced. "Roscoe, are you having a heart attack?"

I heard someone yelling out to call 911, but Roscoe put up a hand and sucked in a deep, ragged breath. He shook his head again. "Sorry," he said. I waited for him to suck in a few more breaths, and then he motioned for me to follow him into the kitchen. Once back there he leaned against the butcher-block table and what he said next shocked me to my core.

"Amy just called. Trey's been murdered."

CHAPTER TWENTY-FIVE

MY TIRES KICKED up an ocean of oyster shells as I peeled out of The Reef's parking lot. Roscoe strapped on his seat belt as I sped around a corner and shot down the Overseas Highway.

Amy and Trey lived in a shotgun house on the north end of the island, and I broke every traffic law there was as I weaved around traffic and floored the pedal. My mind was swirling with questions, and my heart weighed heavy with guilt. After realizing who Trey had gotten into business with, I should have said something. I should have pulled the plug right then and there. But I didn't, and now he was dead.

I could tell Roscoe was trying his best not to cry. The man was a tank, and this would be the first time I ever heard his voice rattle. "What happened, Ryan? Why did this have to happen to Amy?"

"I don't know. But you can believe I'm going to find out."

I turned into the neighborhood and as we pulled up to Amy's house, I saw her sitting in a plastic chair at the foot of her front steps. Roscoe and I jumped out of my truck and ran to her. Her grandfather embraced her in his thick arms, and she sobbed uncontrollably.

I looked up the steps to the open front door. I hated to interrupt the moment, but I put a hand on Amy's shoulder. "Did you call the police?" She nodded. "Listen, you both stay out here and wait for them. If they get here before I come out, tell them a federal agent is already inside." Roscoe waved me on and I slipped out my sidearm and went up the steps.

With Amy already having discovered the body and sitting safely out front these last few minutes, I was fairly certain there was no immediate threat. But the defender in me needed to be sure. The narrow house was painted white, and two ceramic pots filled with growing hibiscus sat on either side of the door. A small metal table and chairs sat off to one side. Overall, it was a simple but practical setup for two younger people just starting their lives.

I leaned over the threshold, scanned the living room, and stepped inside. The entire place had been tossed: couch cushions were on the floor and the television lay on its side; the kitchen drawers had been emptied, and silverware, broken dishes, dry spaghetti noodles, and pot holders were strewn across the floor. The only thing that lay untouched was a circular table encircled with four chairs. Even the pantry had been upended, empty boxes and dry foods spilling out. Vent covers had been yanked off the walls. Clearly someone had come looking for something. I continued down the hall, checking an unused bedroom, its closet and bathroom. It was like an angry tornado had made its way through the home. Proceeding to the bedroom at the end, my throat went dry when I saw Trey's body lying on its side, bleeding out from three bullet wounds in his chest. His skin had already lost its warm tones, conceding to a splotchy blue. After stepping around his body and checking the closet, I went out the back door and stood at the top of the steps. The backyard was tiny and surrounded by a white picket fence in need of a fresh coat of paint. The gate door was open. There didn't appear to be a lock.

Not wanting to disrupt the crime scene, I slowly worked my way back to the front of the house. My chips were on Vargas killing Trey. But of course it was too early to say. I was blind to anyone else Trey might have been working with and why he would have fallen from their graces. Whatever they came looking for, it was clearly important to them.

I holstered my weapon and proceeded down the front steps where Amy was wiping away easy flowing tears with the back of her hand. Roscoe's eyes were rimmed too. I looked to Amy. "Can you tell me what happened?"

Her words came out in a halting fashion as she struggled to get control of herself. "I—I was at The Reef when Trey called me and said he wanted to talk. He said he was sorry for how he'd been acting lately. I was in the middle of the lunch rush so I told him to give me about an hour. I know I messed up a few orders because all I could think about was getting back here and talking with him." She started sobbing again. "Oh, God. What if I would have just come right away? Maybe he wouldn't be dead."

"You can't think like that," Roscoe said. "Odds are you'd probably be dead too."

Sirens sounded in the distance and a minute later a squad car rounded the corner followed by an ambulance. They pulled up beside us and I stepped to the side while Roscoe helped Amy talk with the deputy.

A few minutes later, the street was clogged with emergency vehicles, and curious and concerned neighbors were gathered in a loose cluster on the other side of the crime scene tape. Across the street an unmarked squad car pulled up, and a young man that I'd hoped I'd never see again stepped out. It was Detective Wallace, the sour detective from the motel yesterday.

He crossed the street, and a frown wrinkled his brow as soon as he laid eyes on me. "You?" he scowled. "Why is it that every time I see you, I've got a dead body on my hands?"

"What are you implying, Detective?"

He ignored my question. "What are you doing here?"

"Well, baby face, the victim was a friend of mine." He reddened at my calling him baby face and I got the distinct impression it wasn't the first time someone had used the moniker on him.

"Look," he growled through gritted teeth, "since you're just a friend I'm going to need you to step to the other side of the tape. This isn't your investigation."

I shrugged. "I don't think so. I'm fine right where I am."

"I'm sorry?"

I nodded toward Amy, who was standing next to a hedge with Roscoe still beside her. "She just walked into her house to see her boyfriend shot dead. I'm gonna stay here with her. So do you want to dance the same jig we did last night? Because I think we both know who's going to win again." He rolled his eyes and turned away, silently heading up the steps and disappearing into the house. "Didn't think so," I muttered and then smiled a little.

I decided I wasn't going to tell Wallace about Trey's clandestine meeting on the water the other night. I was certain Vargas or one of his men had done this to Trey. The last thing I needed was for some fresh-faced detective who couldn't tell his head from his ass to misstep and somehow give Vargas a clue that we were on to him.

I looked back to Amy and Roscoe. Both their noses were red, their eyes puffy. I wasn't very good in circumstances like this. I didn't know how to be there for them, or what to say. I knew the best thing I could do right now was to go do my job, to find out who did this and make them pay.

I'd seen more than my share of bodies over the years. Dozens of them during my deployments. The mangled bodies of young kids caught in a crossfire ambush or the path of an enemy IED were the ones that would never leave my mind. And then there was the image of my grandmother as she lay still on her bed, and then of my beloved wife as her broken body was taken away from the accident on a gurney.

I knew the image of Trey lying dead on the floor of his bedroom had seared itself into my memory forever.

And so would the picture of Amy clinging to her grandfather as they both stood shocked and dismayed in the shadow of half a dozen emergency vehicles.

CHAPTER TWENTY-SIX

"WHAT THE HELL, MAN?" I had returned to the office and just finished telling Brad about Trey. "Three rounds to the chest? How's Amy?"

"About how you would expect. She's going to stay with me for a while until we can figure out who did this to Trey, and why."

Brad's fingers curled into fists. "I have a pretty good idea."

"Yeah, well. Whoever killed him—Vargas or not—was looking for something. They trashed the place."

"You think they tried to make it look like it was a home invasion and that Trey just happened to catch them in the act?"

"I thought about that, but with what we know about who Trey was involved with, I seriously doubt it. He had some-thing one of those guys wanted. Even the air duct vents had been unscrewed and removed. That would have taken too much time for someone just looking to stage a detailed robbery."

I slumped in my chair and crossed my arms. With the initial adrenaline spike provided by the murder starting to wear off, I could feel a heavy sense of guilt start to come over me.

"Hey, this isn't your fault," Brad said.

"We knew that Trey was working with some bad people. I should have pushed him harder to talk."

"What time do you want to leave in the morning?"

I sat up straighter and tried to refocus on the investigation at hand. I knew that if we could keep on the right path, following leads and rounding up suspects, eventually it would lead us to Trey's killers. "Daybreak," I replied. "I'll get everything ready tonight. And we're going to find every last person who's moving this money. And we're going to make them pay."

"Damn right we are."

* * *

MY TRUCK ENGINE growled as I turned the corner and pulled up to the front door of The Reef. Amy came out immediately, and I leaned across and opened the passenger door for her. She set a small suitcase on the floor and her pillow on the console. I waited for her to get in and shut the door before turning back out to the road. I knew better than to ask her how she was, so I just said, "We'll find who did it, Amy. I'm sorry I couldn't have stopped it before it happened."

She looked out the window and when she spoke, her voice was weary and sad. "This just doesn't make any sense, Ryan. Who would have wanted him dead? And why? Why do that to Trey, of all people?"

"I don't know," I lied. I just couldn't bring myself to tell her the truth. Not yet, anyway. I didn't know the extent of Trey's involvement with Vargas's organization, and I didn't want to raise even more questions in Amy's anxious mind that I wasn't yet able to answer.

"I mean, what were they looking for?"

"The detectives will look into his murder," I said. And I knew they would. Detective Wallace might be a pain in the ass to deal with on an interagency level, but the county clearly had some confidence in his abilities. "They'll search his emails and social media accounts, check everything on his computer and cell phone. Something's bound to turn up."

We made it back to my boat, and I carried her suitcase into the aft stateroom I had prepared for guests. She would only be the second person to use it. The first had been an old Army buddy who came through a few months ago and stayed a couple days while we caught up and talked of the good old days.

"The bed hasn't been used in a long time," I said, "but the sheets are clean." I showed her where I kept the TV remote and told her that anything in the kitchen pantry was hers. The words were hardly off my tongue when I realized how empty the hospitable gesture actually was.

I didn't keep much food in the place. Some oatmeal, protein powder, a couple bags of chips, and a few pieces of fruit. Most of the time I eat out or order in.

"I'll make a run to the grocery store," I said. "Looks like I'm down to one beer. You want me to pick up more, or something stronger?"

"Rum," she said quickly. "I think a couple shots would help calm my nerves." She rubbed a hand up one of her bare arms like she was cold. "I think I'll go get in the shower. Is that okay?"

"*Mi casa es su casa.*"

After getting some food suggestions, I left her alone and headed toward my truck. The liquor store was the furthest away, so I decided to go there first. When this most recent chaos was over, I was pretty sure we were all going to need our fair share of rum.

CHAPTER TWENTY-SEVEN

IN THE MORNING I woke quietly and brushed my teeth before grabbing a duffle bag full of gear and stepping off the houseboat. The sun was already cresting the horizon over the Atlantic, but Amy was still asleep and I didn't want to wake her. After seeing her boyfriend's dead body yesterday, she needed all the rest she could get. The half-empty bottle of rum on the kitchen counter testified to the fact that she probably wouldn't get out of bed for several more hours, and when she did, it would be with one hell of a hangover.

I wasn't worried about leaving her alone. Vargas didn't know about me and didn't know that I was connected to Trey in any way. It was for that reason that Amy was staying with me and not her grandfather. She would spend her time relaxing on my boat until we got to the bottom of this; no going into work, to Roscoe's, or back to her house. For all we knew, the killer might think that Trey had given Amy what they were looking for and might come looking for her too.

I had gotten with Rich and Edith Wilson last night and informed them about Amy's situation. Since I knew I was going to be gone most of today, I asked them to check up on her a couple times. It was probably good for Amy to be alone, good for her to have the space to grieve the loss of someone she loved, but I also didn't want her feeling isolated.

Once Brad and I got back from Andros Island, I planned on getting in touch with Detective Wallace. I wanted to know what he knew. How Trey got involved with Vargas still wasn't clear, and I wasn't going to rest until all of Amy's questions were answered. If Wallace did find something worthy on Trey's personal electronics, I wanted to know about it.

Every rock would be upturned, every thread pulled and followed until we got to the bottom of this.

Arriving at my Whaler, I stepped on board and unlocked the hatch to the forward lounge. I had prepped our diving gear the night before and quickly performed a final check on the tanks before shutting the hatch again. I didn't know if we'd be using the gear, but my military training had ingrained the need to be prepared into my DNA. Better to be over prepared than to be in a tight spot wishing you had brought along that one piece of equipment.

Setting my duffle bag at my feet, I went aft and untied one of the lines from the dock cleat. The FID had several boats we could use for our day trip. The problem, however, was that some brilliant bureaucrat working with the DoD budget thought it was a good idea to decal the boats' hulls with the Department of Homeland's logo. We weren't the Coast Guard and we weren't the Sheriff's Office; most of what I did as an FID investigator was undercover, so running around announcing who I worked for typically wasn't in the cards.

So we were taking the Whaler.

Brad tossed a leg over the gunwale and untied the remaining lines while I moved behind the helm.

"You check your email this morning?" he asked.

"No," I said. "Why? Did you use my email address to sign yourself up for another sweepstakes?"

"Yeah, but that's not what I'm talking about. Remember when we went and saw Foster up at PortMiami, and he said that Edwards and Holden were last seen taking their yacht around the Caribbean?"

"Yeah."

"Well, we got a hit on their last port of call. A small marina on the south end of Nassau."

"No kidding. Is the yacht still there?"

"No. They said the *Teeming Tuna* came in twenty-three days ago and stayed on its moorings for two nights. They don't have anything else after that. But I figured we could go over and take a look, ask a few questions. Hopefully, we'll get some of their financial information back in the next couple of days and we can start getting an idea of where some of their money was coming from."

"I'm game," I said. The engine growled to life behind me as I turned the key in the ignition.

It looked like it was shaping up to be a very long day.

CHAPTER TWENTY-EIGHT

I⊤ TOOK us just under three hours to get to the central eastern side of Andros Island. Cell service was hit-or-miss, but I'd stopped the boat an hour before when our phones showed a couple bars. There, we checked into customs via an online app and then continued on our course.

There wasn't a cloud in the sky as we approached the large, but relatively uninhabited, Caribbean island. The mid-morning sunlight glinted off the water, and the wind whipped at my face as the boat cut its white trail over the water.

Andros Island consisted of hundreds of small islets and cays connected by tidal swamplands and mangrove estuaries. Less than eight thousand people called the island home, but with the large amount of land, it ended up being less than four people per square mile. Most of the population lived along the edge of Andros City in a communal cluster spanning only a few square miles.

I trimmed our speed and turned into a wide inlet before continuing inland. The channel quickly narrowed and became more shallow, and I started to wonder if maybe Grecko had led us astray with the information he'd provided. Soon enough we came out onto a massive blue hole and I idled the boat across it. Blue holes serve as entrances to intricate water-filled cave systems that run underneath the island and sea floor. Think of them as marine manholes with no lid. They're a diver's paradise, and the best ones attract divers from all over the world.

Thankfully, this one was currently deserted. I had a couple of rods and reels in the forward gunwale and a couple more in the rod holders of the T-top. We both had on long-sleeve T-shirts, ball caps, and wrap-around sunglasses. If anyone spotted us, we would just looked like a couple of anglers cruising the inlets for a place to drop anchor.

I wasn't planning on running into any people out here today. If Grecko had told us the truth, and I was seriously beginning to doubt that he had, then I assumed that the location would have been selected for its secrecy and lay well beyond routes and landmarks typically visited by tourists and nature enthusiasts.

As I slowly moved the boat onward, the water shifted from a dark blue to a light green and then, finally, a clear azure blue. I was just starting to think that, if the location was right, I would need to return in a flat bottom skiff, when Brad pointed out the hull of a large boat sticking out from the mangroves a quarter mile away. I turned into an inlet and went up it as far as I could in order to get out of view of anyone else that might venture in behind us at some point.

Brad had brought one of the drones from the office with him. I dropped anchor and backed down on it. Before I had the engines off, Brad already had the hard case unsnapped and was bringing the drone out from between the molded foam inserts. He set it on the forward deck, brought out the remote, and powered it up.

The boat matched the general location that Grecko had given us. Since he claimed he hadn't been out here yet, he had been unable to give us exact specifics of the location. If he was correct in what he told us, there should be a shack out near the boat.

There were only two ways to get over there. We could either coast right in on the Whaler and wave hello as we came in, or we could come in from above. The drone was whisper quiet and was made with a tempered alloy that allowed the device to blend in with its surroundings—in this case, sky, water, or mangroves. It was Krugman's pet project from last year and was the closest thing to a mechanical chameleon one could find. Once Krugman had uploaded the finished schematics to the Defense Department's servers, the CIA and WARCOM ordered more than a dozen each. It was equipped with infrared, thermal imaging, a 9mm weapons system accurate to 50 yards, and a video camera that would make Hollywood jealous. I'd used it earlier this year to get a recording of a killer Brad and I had tracked through the Glades.

It worked like a charm.

The killer never saw it, never heard it, even though it got within fifteen feet from him in broad daylight. Now he's serving a fifty-year term with no parole.

Brad handed me the remote. It had an eight-inch LED screen that displayed the feed from the camera. We took a step back as the drone's blades came to full speed. A yellow diode on the side switched to green, and I worked the joystick and brought it off the deck. It went up and I moved it over the mangroves and watched it disappear almost immediately into its surroundings. It had a built-in autopilot, so I wasn't worried about accidentally crashing it. Brad looked over my shoulder as I navigated over more islets and thick vegetation. As it neared the boat, a small man-made structure came into view, and a tiny dock connected it to the waterline. The water was darker in the cove, having shifted again from a clear blue to a deep opaque green.

The boat was easily a seventy-five-foot motor yacht, with sleek lines and enormous amounts of deck space below the bridge. I assumed that whoever had brought it in had used an alternate islet from the one we had just come in on. Its draft was probably seven or eight feet, and there was no way it would have made it through the channel my Whaler had brought us in by.

I circled the drone around and zoomed in on the vessel. The blinds were drawn over the galley's windows, and I could see no one in the forward salon. The thermal imaging picked up nothing but sunlight.

I moved on to the shack, which looked like it was made of new pine boards and no larger than my houseboat. The wood was painted a camo blend of greens and grayish browns, which helped it to blend right into its surroundings. A large generator sat behind the shack draped in camo netting.

"Well, whatever this is, they're trying to hide it," Brad mused out loud. "Is it picking up any sound?"

I toggled over to the audio reading and nothing but the breeze showed on the display. I directed the audio stream toward the bottom of the front door and still got nothing. No conversation or electronics. The generator was not currently running.

I returned my attention to the boat and spent the next couple of minutes trying to determine if anyone was on board. The vessel would have several staterooms and as good as it was, the drone wouldn't be able to give us a clear enough reading deep inside. I was just about to pull back on the joystick and bring it back in when I decided to get a reading on the name and hailing port. I dropped the drone several feet and pointed the camera towards the hull. My heart started beating a little faster. I could feel a fresh excitement pumping through my body.

"Am I reading that right?" Brad said, still looking over my shoulder. "Is that what I think it is?"

"Yeah. Looks like we hit the jackpot with our first scratch off."

"I'll be damned."

The watercraft was the *Teeming Tuna*. Holden's missing yacht.

CHAPTER TWENTY-NINE

I QUICKLY BROUGHT the drone back and Brad started packing it away while I brought out the dive gear.

"You sure you want to go over there?" he said. "It might be better to wait until they're expecting Grecko and descend on them then."

"We're here now," I said. "I want to know what's in that shack and what might be on that boat. If there's someone over there and they see us, we can just play dumb and act like a couple of lost divers."

Today, our mission was simply surveillance: observe and see if we could come away with any new faces or information. Grecko was scheduled to be back in four days with his Bahamian passport in hand. That's when we would return with backup and hopefully start making some arrests.

Good men had died down in Guatemala. Trey was dead. And now that we knew the Barker investigation was tied into all Gallardo's money I was ready to start shutting things down.

We donned our gear, shouldered our tanks. I didn't expect to go down past fifteen feet on this dive, so I left my BCD vest on the deck. I would just regulate my buoyancy by breathing. I slipped my mask over my face and popped my regulator into my mouth before slipping into the water. Brad waited for me to move away from the boat before getting into the water and swimming in behind me.

We finned back down the inlet, through water that was as transparent as a resort's swimming pool—horizontal visibility was well over a hundred feet. When we reached the main tributary, we hooked left and started for the cove. We were there in less than five minutes and the water immediately became murkier, darker, which was just to my liking. The last thing I wanted was for someone to come out onto the yacht's deck and start using us for target practice.

We kept on the along the cove's perimeter until I felt one of the dock's pilings beneath my hand. I slowly surfaced and came up under the relative privacy of the small dock. I removed my mask and popped out my regulator just as Brad came up with me.

A few large rocks protruded off the land and into the water. I shed my tank and set it across where the rocks came under the dock but above the water line. Then I removed my fins and, with a final look around, grabbed at a few of the mangrove roots near my legs and quickly worked my way out of the water.

Moving stealthily, I quickly made my way to the front door of the shack and pressed my ear against the door. Hearing nothing, I placed my fingers around the handle and turned it. Surprisingly, it gave way behind my hand and I slowly pushed open the door and peered inside. No lights were on, but enough sunlight was coming from a small window in the back.

The place was vacant.

There was a wire-framed bed with a flimsy mattress on it and a small table with two wooden chairs in the corner. I lifted the mattress and inspected the floorboards for something that would cause me to think there was a hidden storage compartment. I didn't find anything. The place seemed pretty straightforward. I don't know what kind of living arrangements Grecko thought he would be walking into but this setup was about as lonely as it could get.

I exited the shack and slipped back into the water. At this point I doubted that anyone was on the yacht. A part of me wanted to board it, but the more reasonable part didn't want to risk a premature engagement. We were finally making headway on this investigation, and the last thing I wanted to do was scare off whoever was behind all this.

"I got the tracker on the hull of the yacht," Brad said.

"Good deal." I got my dive gear back on. "Ready to go back?"

"Yep."

We dove and headed back without incident. I climbed up the dive ladder at the transom, and after peeling off my gear, I went to check the time on my phone.

I had seven missed calls from the office.

CHAPTER THIRTY

I WAS ABOUT to tap the number to call it back when my phone rang in my hand. "Hello?"

"Ryan! Geez, where the hell have you been?" It was Spam, our IT guy.

"Doing something called working. We're out in the field."

"Okay, whatever. So you got a minute?" All frustration was suddenly gone from his voice, and he sounded like he had just scored a date with a supermodel.

"For you, sure, Spam. What's up?" I brought the phone away from my ear and put the call on speaker so Brad could hear.

"Okay. So. The USB drive Brad gave me yesterday. I know you guys wanted me to try to make sense of that long number in the Excel spreadsheet."

"Any luck?"

"No. Well—yes. I mean, not in the way you thought. Ryan, the file had a hidden tab."

"A hidden tab? You can do that?"

"Of course you can do that! You just format it through the visibility functions." He said it like I had just insinuated that I didn't know what a keyboard was.

"So what did you find?"

"What did I find? Man, there was a hyperlink embedded into one of the cells and it led to an unlisted, password-protected web page."

Brad leaned in and spoke. "Could you hack into it?"

"No! I didn't need to. The password was that long number that you were trying to get me to crack."

Brad and I looked at each other and then back to the phone.

"So," Spam continued, "you won't believe what the webpage leads to."

"We're listening."

"It leads back to a cluster of files on the dark web. Basically, the files are hidden on a virtual shelf that no one can access except through the way I just did."

"So what did you find?"

"Right. So I'm not exactly sure what you were hoping for but I've got banking records. Lots of banking records between several different accounts in the Caymans and two in Switzerland. The accounts belong to a few people. Jim Barker, Tina Edwards, and Steve Holden. Then there's one for an Ian Foster as well. It looks like he runs a container refurbing business up in PortMiami. But Foster's account is empty and hasn't seen any transactions in the last couple of months."

Finally, we had the money trail. And it seemed like Foster was telling us the truth about walking the straight and narrow since Barker was arrested.

"Spam," I said. "Can you email it to me? And CC Kathleen and Brad on it too."

"I'm uploading it all to the FID Dropbox account. You should have access to it all within the next five minutes. But Ryan, there's more. A location keeps coming up in all these files. It's out on Cay Sal Bank. Whatever these guys are up to, I'm pretty sure they're doing something important from the Bank."

I thanked Spam for his good work and we hung up. "I'll bet that info is what Barker was going to give to the DEA to make his deal with them," I said. "Somehow Scahill came across it and knew what he had."

"Or Scahill knew all along," Brad said. "And he's the one who killed Barker to get it. You wanna roll over to Cay Sal Bank and see what we can see? Should only take us a couple hours to get there from here."

I lifted the seat to the forward lounge and started stowing our dive gear. "Let's do it."

CHAPTER THIRTY-ONE

WHEN AMY AWOKE on Ryan's houseboat it took her a few moments to remember where she was.

And why?

Yesterday's events came crashing over her like a living nightmare, and it took everything she had not to curl back under the covers and shut the world out again. When she sat up, she was reminded just how much rum she'd had the night before. Her head was pounding and her mouth was as dry as parchment paper. She slowly stood up and went into the bathroom. After brushing her teeth, she went into the galley and downed two tall glasses of water and a couple of Advil that she found in a kitchen drawer.

She couldn't get the image of Trey's lifeless body out of her mind. It was stuck there and nothing she tried would make it go away. She sat on the couch for a while and when the headache started to wane, she got back up and returned to her stateroom. The suitcase she'd brought with her was still standing in the corner. She walked over to it, tossed it on the bed, and unzipped it. A chest of drawers sat against the bulkhead behind her and she figured, if she was going to be here for a while, that she might as well go ahead and unpack.

After removing the bulk of her clothing, she unzipped an inside pocket and reached in for her makeup bag. But when her fingers touched the bottom, she felt something unfamiliar. She latched onto it and lifted it out.

It was a small spiral notebook. Lifting back the front cover, she started scanning the words on the first page, and then flipped to the next, and then the next, her astonished eyes growing larger with every word.

It was all in Spanish, but Amy had taken two semesters of Spanish up in Gainesville. She wasn't fluent by any means, but she knew enough to make sense of what she was reading. After several pages she realized that *this* was what Trey's killer had been looking for. She started to feel dizzy. Reaching out for the wall. she grabbed at it to steady herself. After taking a few deep breaths, she sat down on the bed and continued to study the pages, hardly blinking until she had read them all.

It clicked. The scribbles and annotations on the notepad provided all the missing pieces. What Trey had been doing was perfectly clear now.

She grabbed her purse and started rummaging for the business card Detective Wallace had given her. Finding it, she grabbed her phone from the nightstand and dialed. He answered after several rings.

"Wallace."

"Detective, this is Amy Green, Trey Stewart's girlfriend."

"What can I help you with, Miss Green?"

"I—I've just found a small notebook. I think it might be what Trey's killers were looking for."

"A notebook? What's in it?"

"Names, locations, and it looks like tallies of products they're selling. But the products are abbreviated. I can't make sense of them. Where can I meet you so I can get it to you?"

"I'm on vacation for the next three days. If you want, you can drop it off at my office with Detective Cooper. He'll keep it safe until I return to the office."

Vacation? "I'm sorry, you're saying someone won't even take a look at this until you get back?"

"That's what I'm saying. If you want—"

Amy hung up on him in a rage. What kind of moron detective was this guy? She navigated to the favorites in her contacts and dialed Ryan.

No answer. It just kept ringing. She tried again. "Come on..." After the third time, she tried calling Brad and immediately got his voicemail.

"Unbelievable," she muttered. She paced the room for several minutes as she thought through the information in the notebook. Finally, she grabbed a fresh change of clothes and put them on. Then, with her face set in a steely resolve, she grabbed her keys from a drawer in the galley and headed out.

She could play detective too.

CHAPTER THIRTY-TWO

AFTER WORKING our way out of the tight circuitry of inlets and getting back into open water, I hit the throttle and brought the Whaler up on plane as I headed north toward Andros Town. We arrived there in under half an hour, and I pulled into the marina and filled the boat with gas. Brad took the opportunity to grab us some fish tacos and lobster rolls from a street vendor. Once we and the boat were topped off, we took off again beneath the bright rays of the Caribbean sun.

Cay Sal Bank is a huge atoll covering an area over two thousand square miles, only a quarter of which is dry land. It's situated seventy miles southeast of Key Largo and nearly a hundred miles off the western coast of Andros Island. Think of an enormous triangle with everything but its outer edge beneath the water. Rather than sand-hemmed islands, what's above the water are mostly small cays and craggy rock islands, all of which are unlivable for humans; most areas resembled nothing more than a rock-formed jetty. About the only visitors to the remote area are scuba divers looking to explore its incredible blue holes and virgin coral reefs.

It could make a perfect rendezvous for smugglers.

I glanced at my Garmin and adjusted my course on our approach. Looking out to the horizon, I could just make out a crag of rocks as they reflected the midday sunlight.

The last thing I wanted to do was to announce to whoever might be over there that they had visitors, so I cut an arc to the south end of the cay so the higher rocks would hide our approach. I set the anchor and cut the engines a mile and a half out, and Brad put up the diver down flag.

I reached for the duffle I'd brought with me and unzipped it. I brought out two Glocks and the binoculars and transferred them to a waterproof pouch. Then I removed my shoes and put them in the bag too. I tossed Brad another waterproof bag.

"I've got your weapon, but I'm not carrying your stupid shoes."

"Probably a good idea," he said. "I was even offended when I took them off last night. I think it's time to throw them in the wash."

We geared up and I strapped the bag to my chest. Brad did the same with his. I looked down at the drone's case sitting near my feet, thinking of a way we could bring it. Our waterproof bags weren't large enough for it to fit, and the case wasn't fully watertight.

"Same plan?" he said. "We come across someone and we're just lost divers?"

"I think if there's something going on out here it's pretty big. I'm not sure we'll be able to talk our way out. Let's just make sure no one sees us. So how about not whistling any Billy Ray while we're out here."

He sighed. "Fine. But only because I don't like getting shot at." He stepped to the transom and entered the water. Once he was a safe distance away, I made a giant stride entry and splashed in behind him.

The water depth was forty feet. This wasn't a pleasure dive, so we only descended to twelve feet. All we needed was to mask our approach to the strip of land we thought might harbor smugglers looking to bring in counterfeit money into the U.S.

I had set anchor where the water was a deep, stunning blue, but the closer we got to the cay, it became more shallow and clearer. I looked down on a low-profile reef teeming with Atlantic spadefish, queen angelfish, and green moray eels, the latter of which I never had grown super comfortable around. Their yellow-green skin, tapered head, and beady eyes seemed to convey evil intent, in spite of their docile tendencies.

The reef rose up to meet us as we neared the cay, and I located a sandy break where we came up out of the water. I grabbed onto a limestone outcropping and spit out my regulator out as I threw my right leg on top of the rocky ledge and slid over so Brad could join me. A thick growth of sea grapes grew up behind us and we shed our diving gear, put on our shoes, and performed a quick press check on our Glocks. I pulled out the binoculars and peered through the covering of sea grapes and turned my attention down the cay.

The rocky stretch of land was no more than a half mile long and fifty yards across at its widest. It was mostly flat, with some areas where the rocks rose higher and a mangrove or two stuck out. My eyes finally landed on a man-made structure tucked into the shade of a higher rock face. Much like the shack we had seen out on Andros Island, it was painted to blend in with its surroundings.

"There's something down there," I said. "Let's get closer in and see if we can get a better idea of the setup."

"Wish we had the drone," Brad said. "The last thing we need is for someone to see us."

We ducked low as we slipped out of cover and advanced across the flat, rocky ground. Every ten or twenty feet we had to hop over a large fissure that led straight down to the water. The cay had to be home to dozens of small caves.

A perfect place to hide contraband.

We pulled up and ducked behind a small mangrove when we heard a voice on the wind. I brought out the binoculars again and searched the area around the small building. A man's head came into view. I could only see the back of it and nothing below the shoulders. I followed his path toward the water and soon noticed a boat's T-top in the distance. The boat was tied up to the cay.

"You hear that?" Brad said.

I paused and listened. "No."

"What, are you deaf? Listen again."

Then I heard it. The distinctive drone of an outboard engine, coming in from the west. I shifted my focus toward the open stretch of water to my left and quickly found the boat. It was a center console moving toward us at top speed. I focused in on the person behind the wheel.

My whole body froze. "What the——?"

"What?" Brad asked. "Who is it?"

"Sonofabitch," I said and brought the glasses away from my face. I shook my head in disbelief. "It's Amy."

CHAPTER THIRTY-THREE

"What?" Brad snatched the glasses from my hands and peered through them. He swore under his breath. "What in the hell, man? What's she doing here?" He turned to look at me. "You don't think she's in on all this, do you? You think—you think she killed Trey?"

"Not a chance," I said. "She's a good kid."

He nodded to her approaching boat. "Then how do you explain that?"

"I don't know, but I sure plan on finding out. Come on."

Ducking again, we hurried forward and stopped behind a large limestone boulder. We peered out, watching as Amy slowed on her approach. She didn't seem to have a direct bearing, liked she wasn't quite sure where she was going. I looked down the cay to where I had seen the man's head earlier. He was on his boat now, and I heard the engines start up and watched the boat come into full view as he pulled away from land. He cut north and rounded the north end of the cay before cutting a path toward Amy.

Having no idea what she was doing out here, I was half-expecting Amy to move toward the other boat. But as soon as she saw it, she immediately turned and headed away from the cay, back into open water. I couldn't get a clear view of her face but everything in me said she was scared, that the other boat had been unexpected, as well as the man on it.

With three 300 HP outboards on the transom, his boat was much faster, and he gained easily. I continued watching through the binoculars as he yelled something at her. When she answered by turning the boat out, he reached behind him and tugged a handgun from the back seam of his shorts.

"Oh, no."

He fired two shots. One hit the hull of her boat and the other missed wide. Amy screamed and kept her speed while trying to out maneuver him.

A flash of hot anger ran through me, and my knuckles turned white as I tightened my grip on my pistol. They were out of range; there was nothing I could do from over here.

"This completely changes the game," Brad said. "We need to call this in ASAP. The Coast Guard and FBI need to be out here, like, yesterday. Looks like you and I dropped the ball on this one. A couple professionals we are."

He was referring to the fact that, with all the gear we brought along, we had failed to pack an extra radio. Now the only way to communicate to the outside world was via the radio in our boat. Since our cell phones had no service out here we had left them on the boat.

I suddenly felt something I wasn't used to while on the job: helplessness. Somehow Amy had stumbled into the hornet's nest and from where I stood right now, I could do nothing but watch as a helpless spectator.

Up ahead I could hear several men barking at each other in Spanish. "Come on," I said. "We need to see if there's another boat up here. We've got to find a fast way to get out to Amy."

By showing ourselves we would compromise the mission and possibly everything we had worked for up to this point. But saving Amy's life had now become the priority. Brad followed me out from the cover of the boulder and we charged across the rocky surface with our weapons firmly in our grasp. Up ahead the ground suddenly dropped off toward the water line. I stopped at the edge and looked down into a small cove. We were standing at the top of a cliff face that ended thirty feet below at a narrow strip of beach. Four men that looked of Spanish descent were running toward another boat anchored at the edge of the cove. One of them spotted us and shouted at the others, two of whom had semi-automatic rifles in their hands.

Altering their course, they turned toward us and Brad and I hit the deck as a volley of bullets hit the cliff and whizzed over our heads. I rolled over behind a rock the size of a large pumpkin and started returning fire. One of my rounds caught a man in the thigh and he dropped in the shallow water, howling. The other three ran across the sand toward the cliff face and disappeared from view.

I looked to Brad, who was wiping a bead of sweat from his brow. "Nice fellas," he said.

"You could have shot one."

Keeping my gun trained below, I came to my knees and craned my neck to survey the area around the cove. It was quiet, and I came to the quick conclusion that a cave of some sort was below us. Brad and I were probably on top of it.

Just as I was debating how to strategically move from our position, a loud scuffle came from behind me. I realized too late that someone had snuck up from below, probably up from a hidden crevice in the rock face. I tensed and turned, swinging my gun around to face my attacker. But I was too late. A rifle butt hit me square in the forehead. I pitched backward, the back of my head slamming into the rock, and everything went black.

CHAPTER THIRTY-FOUR

WHEN I CAME TO, I had one of those rare experiences when you don't exactly remember where you are. Like the morning after meeting a girl at a bar and going home with her—that first moment when you open your eyes and smell fried bacon, but look around the bedroom and don't recognize the pink sheets or the perfume bottles on the hutch. It was *that* feeling. On top of that, my head was pounding like I'd polished off a fifth of whiskey.

Brad's voice came from somewhere out in front of me. "Welcome back. I was thinking maybe you were going to sleep through all fun." He sounded tired.

I raised my chin off my chest and blinked most of the blurriness away. We were in a room with an old stone floor, rubbed smooth by decades, if not centuries of wear. The rough stone walls were formed with ancient mortar, and I recognized this as the building we observed on our way in. A small stone-framed opening acted as a window and let in the bright sunlight. I could hear the ocean slapping against the rocks below.

I couldn't speak. My mouth was wrapped in duct tape and I had to focus not to suffocate as I sucked air through the one nostril that wasn't clogged with drying blood. My hands were bound tightly behind my back, my ankles tethered to wooden chair legs.

Brad was sitting on the floor in front of me, leaning against the wall. He smiled at me and nodded to an empty roll of tape on the floor near my feet. He shrugged. "They ran out of duct tape. Not really sure why they wanted to wrap your mouth like a Christmas present. There isn't anyone to hear us for fifty miles."

I tried to think past the pressure squeezing my brain. With the way I was currently tied up, there wasn't any way to get enough leverage to break the chair against the floor. Brad was clearly thinking the same thing. "I've almost got my hands loose," he said. "There's a rough part of stone right under my ankles. I've already got the ropes cut."

I looked at his feet. The ropes were still wrapped around his ankles. From my point of view it looked like they were still secure.

Amy running her boat away from the cay drifted across my vision, and I tensed.

We'd failed her.

I had no idea what happened or where she might be.

An old wooden door opened on my right and a man with a hooked nose and dark hair oiled back against his scalp walked into the room and stood in front of me.

"I knew it was you," Brad snapped. "You're a real piece of work."

Carlos Vargas smiled broadly, like he was reacting to a joke. "So you have it all figured out, do you?"

"Before all this is over," Brad said through gritted teeth, "I'm going to wrap my fingers around your throat and strangle you with my own hands."

"Why?" Vargas scoffed. "Because I tied you up like you were a wild pig?"

"No, because you killed Trey Stewart. And where the hell is Amy?"

"Oh, my friend." Vargas chuckled. "I did not kill Trey. Although, I did not like him much, or trust him."

"Yeah? Then who did?"

The door opened again. Three men stepped into the small room. Two Spanish-looking men came and stood behind me. The third one stopped behind Vargas. I raised my chin and tried to get a look but was unable to see him.

"I'm afraid *I'm* the one who killed Trey Stewart," the newcomer said. "He was a loose string I just couldn't afford any longer."

My eyes widened and my body tensed hard against my restraints. I knew that voice.

Knew it well in fact.

It was that of Secret Service Special Agent Bud Cole.

CHAPTER THIRTY-FIVE

"You?" Brad said. "Aren't you—"

"Yes," Cole interrupted. "Yes, I am."

"You killed Trey?" Brad growled. "Why?"

"Simple, really. I've had a crew moving money up from South America for the last six months. I pushed for the Secret Service to go hard after Gallardo and get him shut down. And it worked. With the help of two other U.S. agencies, we got him. And all that money was just there for the taking."

"So you planned the attack on Gallardo's mansion and set fire to it?"

"It's quite amazing what poor people down there are willing to do for the promise of a little money." He looked to his bad shoulder, which was still in a sling. "We had to make it look real." He smiled. "Trey was simply running passports and forged legal paperwork to us so we could get some of our men into the U.S. After Barker got shut down, we had to find another way to move the product."

"So you're the one who called Ian Foster and told him to start outfitting new containers for you?"

Cole seemed momentarily surprised that Brad was privy to such information. "Yes."

"And you killed Scahill too? In his hotel room?"

"No," Vargas said, "that was me." He turned to me and lifted his middle finger to me, just like he had when he escaped from me on the skiff a few days before.

Cole looked to me. "My conversation with you at The Reef was simply an attempt to feel you out and see if you were on to any of us. I remember you telling me in Guatemala that you were working a case involving a Jim Barker."

I'd seen a lot of things in my day, but this took the cake. The level of secrecy and manipulation it would have taken Cole to pull something like this off was extraordinary.

Cole's phone dinged in his pocket. He pulled it out and looked at a text. I had no idea how he was getting service out here. He smiled and typed out a quick reply. At the same moment, I locked eyes with Brad. If there was to be a moment that we were getting out of this, it was now. Brad shifted his weight and moved slowly off his hands. Then, like a panther after his prey he sprang into action, jumping to his feet as he flung the ropes aside and lunged at Cole. Only fifteen feet stood between the two men, but Cole reacted with lightning-fast reflexes. Almost as if he'd been expecting something, Cole reached for his sidearm, pointed it directly at Brad, and fired off two quick rounds.

I watched in horror, screaming through the tape across my mouth, as my best friend took both 9mm rounds in the chest and crumbled lifelessly to the ground, landing at the feet of the dirty Secret Service Agent.

Cole stared at down at Brad and cocked his head to the side. "Fast little sonofabitch, wasn't he?" He shrugged and looked to me. "How about you, Savage? Want to take a run at me?"

My eyes bore into his, converting every ounce of hatred I felt for the man.

I had to pull my eyes away. I thought I might suffocate, still able to suck air through only one unclogged nostril. Watching Brad get murdered right in front of me got my heart pumping like I'd just run the hundred yard dash. I felt like I was going to pass out. Cole holstered his gun. "I'll let you think about what just happened for a little while. After that I'll come back to see if you're in the mood to give me a little more information. I need to know everything that the Federal Intelligence Directorate knows about this little operation we have going on here. And how you found out about this place. For now, though, I'm going to let Manuel and Ramiro here have their way with your lady friend in that back room there. What's her name? Amy? Ramiro especially likes the pink highlights."

I felt a vein pulse across my forehead, and I clenched my fists harder than they already were. I looked up at him and growled madly through my gag. Everything in me wanted to burst out of the chair and shove my thumbs into his eye sockets.

Cole nodded to his men and I heard them shuffle through another door behind me. Cole laughed to himself and exited the room through the side door he had entered just minutes before. Vargas followed after and shut the door behind him. I turned my attention back to Brad. My eyes teared up as I stared at his dead body, sprawled out across the dirty stone floor, the two bullet holes leaking blood from his chest. Behind me, Amy released a blood-curdling scream.

They were going to put her through hell.

And there wasn't a damn thing I could do about it.

CHAPTER THIRTY-SIX

THE SOUND of clothing tearing in the other room made my blood boil. Amy screamed again, and then I heard the clear slap of an open palm against a cheek. She went quiet.

I saw a shudder of movement in front of me and looked to see Brad's left arm slide slowly over the floor from his side toward his head. He was alive. Maybe not for long. But for now, he was, and I tried yelling at him through my gag, but it only came out at an angry muffle. All of a sudden, he started dragging himself toward me. The side of his face was sliding across the floor, but he said weakly, "Shut..up. You...sound like—like...*a bitch.*"

I shook my head in disbelief and watched as Brad slowly crawled toward me. His face was contorted in pain, and he looked more dead than alive. Most of his shirt was soaked with blood, his eyes nearly glazed over, his breath raspy. I knew he was in shock. He should be dead—moments ago I thought he was—and if we couldn't find a way out of this soon and get him to a doctor, there was no way he was going to make it to tomorrow.

He was only a couple of feet from me now, and I tried twisting in the chair so I could bring my wrists closer to him. It didn't do much good; my range of motion was almost nil. But the chair did swivel a few inches and soon enough I felt his fingers moving over the ropes that were binding my wrists.

Come on.

I felt some pressure give and blood rush back into my hands. He grunted and fell back. I yelled again, trying to spur him on.

Come ON.

A few seconds later, I felt his fingers moving again and the final knot gave away enough for me to slip my hands free. I immediately leaned over and worked my ankles loose, tossing the ropes away as I stood up and kneeled down beside him. "Don't move anymore," I said. "Hang tight. I'll get you out of this." He was about to say something when his eyes rolled back into his head and he passed out.

There was nothing I could do for him and no one else around to hold pressure on his wounds. So, knowing that his life was slipping away, I sprang into action, a deep-seated fury fueling my every move.

I quickly scanned the room for any kind of weapon—a board, a rock, or even a discarded nail. There was nothing. As I rushed toward the back room, I figured I would have the element of surprise. Manuel and Ramiro would be giving her their full attention.

Wrapping my fingers around the handle, I flung the door open and charged inside. My stomach curled at what I saw. They had Amy on the bed, one man kneeling beside her with a blade on her throat. The other one was standing at her feet, trying to yank her shorts off. Her shirt was gone, but thankfully her bra remained intact.

Both men still had their shorts on, but their shirts off, and their backs to me. The one at Amy's feet had a fixed-blade knife sheathed at his side. Before he could turn and see who had burst through the door, I had my hand on the hilt of his knife. I snatched it out just as the other man removed his blade from Amy and lunged toward me. I shot my leg out and my foot connected to his chest. The force of the impact threw him backwards, and he tumbled off the bed and fell haphazard onto the floor.

Amy belted out another scream.

Gripping the knife, I locked eyes with the man standing disoriented beside me, then swung the knife around, plunging the long blade straight into his throat. His body shuddered from the impact of the blow, and his hands went up and grabbed my wrists as he struggled for breath, blood now pouring down his chest. I yanked the blade free and shoved him to the side while I turned my attention to the man just clamoring up from the floor.

He was on his feet now, his blade glistening in the ceiling light. He was short, but his tattooed arms were corded with lean muscle, and he grinned like he was ready for a good fight. I stepped forward in an effort to get him to retreat farther away from Amy. It worked, and he took a couple of cautious steps back. Amy used that as an opportunity to roll across the bed and her feet found the floor on the other side. She stood there cowering, stunned by the events of the last several minutes.

My opponent raised his knife and slashed out in a downward diagonal motion. All he cut was air. I shuffled back and out of the way as the blade passed by, and as his forward motion carried his hand toward the floor, I repositioned my weight, turned, and executed a near-perfect back kick. My heel punched into his solar plexus, lifted his entire body off the floor, and sent him careening into the wall.

I stepped up, tightened my grip on my blade, and raked it across his face. His cheek and nose opened up in a bloody trough, and he cried out in pain. But it was short lived, stopped suddenly by my blade puncturing his diaphragm. I stepped in and pushed hard, shoving him against the wall. His mouth yawed up and down as he tried to breathe. I twisted the knife and looked him deep in the eyes as the life slowly drained from him. Leaning in, I whispered in his ear. "This is why you don't violate women." Then I yanked my knife free and he crumpled to the floor, lifeless.

One of the men's T-shirts was lying on the back of a chair near the bed. I grabbed it and quickly wiped some of the men's blood off my hands before tossing it to the side and moving over to Amy. I wrapped my arms around her shaking body. "Are you okay?"

She didn't answer, just kept shaking. "Come on," I said. "We've gotta get out of here." Turning, I found her shirt on the floor and held it out to her. She quickly put it on and folded her arms tightly against her chest. "Brad's been shot," I told her. "We need to move fast. Whatever happens, from here on out, stay right behind me at all times."

When she nodded her head that she understood, I bent down and quickly searched the pockets of the dead men for a cell phone: *nothing*. I had to get the Coast Guard out here for Brad or he wasn't going to make it. I wiped the knife blade on the bed, centered it in my palm, and then looked to Amy. "Ready?"

"Yes," she said quietly.

I moved through the doorway and back to the room where Brad lay unmoving on the floor. Amy threw a hand to her mouth, forgetting her own problems for the moment. "Oh my God," she whispered and choked out a sob. I kneeled down beside Brad and set two fingers on his neck. His pulse was faint—almost nonexistent. "I've got to find a phone," I said. "Or a radio. We've got to get him off this rock."

Amy looked toward the door that led out of here. "I'm going to kill that man with my bare hands," she growled.

"Amy," I said. "You need to stay here with Brad."

"What? Ryan, no. I'm not—"

"Amy. If he stops breathing, you're going to have to give him CPR. If you're not here, he could die. I have to find a way to let someone know where we are and stop Cole." I set my hand on her shoulder and looked her in the eyes. "Okay?"

She nodded unsurely, the recent trauma clearly evident in her eyes. "Okay."

I stood up and returned to the back room where I'd found her. Stepping over the body of the second man I'd killed, I reached down and grabbed his knife. Thankfully the growing pool of blood on the floor hadn't run up to it yet. I came back to Amy and put the knife in her hand. "When I come back, I'll rap on the door three times and say my name. So don't stab me when I come back in. Anyone else, you put that through their heart. You hear me?"

"Yes," she said. And then her body straightened and her chin rose slightly. When she spoke again, her voice was stronger and filled with resolve. "Yes," she said again. "Now go get those monsters."

Clutching my own knife, I headed toward the door. "That's the plan."

This all ended right now.

CHAPTER THIRTY-SEVEN

I WAS TEMPORARILY BLINDED by the bright sunlight as I stepped back outside. The stone building sat near the edge of the narrow cay tucked against a wall of rock, and a series of stone steps snaked away and descended toward the cliff, leading to the water below. From my vantage point, I had a partial view of the cove below. A small fishing boat was pulling away from the sandy shore and, much to my pleasure, Cole and Vargas were not on it. They watched the boat breach the cove's outer perimeter and enter the deeper blue waters of the Atlantic before turning and walking back across the sand to the base of the steps.

I quickly moved to the far wall of the building and used it for cover as I watched the two men ascend. The top of the cliff hid them from view for a few seconds, and the next glimpse I got was of Vargas continuing upwards without Cole. He never did reappear and when Vargas reached the top, he headed for the building. My desire for revenge ticked higher with every step he took toward me.

I waited until he was just feet from the front door before making my move and springing out from behind the wall. Vargas was caught completely off guard, surely thinking that I was still tied up inside. Before he could reach for his gun, I was already behind him, a hand gripping his wrist, my knife's blade at his throat. He froze and winced as the pressure from the blade dug into his flesh. I could smell the musky odor of the oil he used in his hair.

"Your two buddies inside," I said. "They're a bloody mess. Want to guess why?"

He didn't bother to answer.

"Let's start with that boat," I said. "Where was it going?"

"East Bimini. A marina called the Sea Tortoise."

"Does the boat have a name?"

"*Green Lady.*"

"Where's Cole?" I put more pressure on the knife, and he winced again as it bit deeper into his flesh.

"There's—there's a small cave down the steps. He's in there finishing inventory of the money."

"Does he have a radio with him?"

"What?"

"A radio, you idiot. Is there a radio in there?"

"Yes—yes. There's a radio." For now, that was all I needed to know.

With a single swift motion, I removed the blade off of Vargas's throat, stepped back, and brought the butt of the knife around, sending it into the back of Vargas's head. He grunted and crumbled to the ground, unconscious. Vargas might be a bastard, but killing in cold blood wasn't in my wheelhouse. He was going to stand trial and answer for his crimes. Besides, bringing a warm body home would make Kathleen happy, and I still had a little ground to make up with her.

Cole, on the other hand, was different. What he had done was far more personal. He had admitted to personally killing Trey and had given his men permission to violate Amy. He wasn't making it off this rock alive. All I had to do was engage him, wait for him to come after me, and then killing him would be fair game. Amy and Trey would have their justice today.

Beside me, a run of railroad vines spread out over the rocks, their bright pink flowers in full bloom. I grabbed a length of the long viny shoots and tore them away from the earth, then sliced the knife's blade across it. A three foot length fell into my hand. After cutting off another length I took the vines and bound Vargas's hands and feet. Just for spite, I cut off his shirt and left him to burn in the sun.

Then I snatched up his gun, checked the load, and went off to hunt Cole.

CHAPTER THIRTY-EIGHT

THE STONE STEPS were slick with moisture. I moved cautiously down them, keeping the gun trained out in front of me. A landing appeared on my right—a wide ledge that led up to the mouth of a cave. The cave was large enough for a small car to pass into but certainly not high enough for any regularly sized adult to enter without ducking.

I stepped onto the landing and looked down. The cove's sandy beach lay just ten feet below. Another fishing boat was anchored just off a jut of rocks.

That boat would have a radio in it, and I needed to notify someone of our situation and get help for Brad. I'd left him alone with Amy just minutes ago, but for all I knew, he could already be gone. Brad was tough, and for all his light-hearted humor, deep down he was still a battle-hardened Marine. But it would take everything he had to fight through this until help arrived.

I needed to get that boat's radio, but I needed to take out Cole first. The last thing I wanted was for Cole to come out of that cave and see me down below. I'd be a sitting duck with no means of decent cover.

I started advancing on the cave, looking for signs of any movement inside.

With every step my anger burned hotter. Cole had been a trusted agent, sworn to protect America's national security and its interests. But he had betrayed his oath, and now many good men were dead because of it. All because of his own selfish greed.

My advance was suddenly stopped by two bullets raking by my face and slamming to the rock wall beside me. As the shots echoed inside the cave, I turned on my heel and bolted back to the steps and the cover of the narrow walkway. Cole's voice sounded from the darkness of the cave. "Well, look at you, Savage! How'd you break out of your cage?"

Lifting my gun, I returned fire, sending three rounds into the mouth of the cave. I was firing blindly, having no idea where he was. He couldn't be too far in. I hadn't seen any indication that he was using a flashlight of any kind. Cole had to be near enough to the cave's entrance to use the natural light spilling in from outside.

"Missed!" he called out tauntingly.

"You're not making it off this rock alive, Cole!"

His prideful laugh echoed out into the daylight. "Then come and get me! I'm right here!"

I could see no more than five feet inside the cave, after that only a thick darkness. There was no way for me to advance on it; I'd be target practice. I was agile and quick, but I wasn't stupid. A scuffing sound emanated from the cave, and I assumed that Cole had gotten back to work, probably moving around boxes of money.

Going forward wasn't an option, and Brad didn't have time for me to work through a Mexican standoff. I could only think of one additional scenario.

I stepped around the corner and returned a foot to the ledge, squeezing off three rounds before turning and bolting up the stairs as fast as I could. I was back at the top of the cay in seconds. I ran past the building where Amy and Brad were and drew up where I knew the roof of the cave to be. My only hope was to find a fissure in the roof of the cave that might give me clandestine access from above.

I was quickly rewarded.

Beneath a run of railroad vines was a crack only slightly more than two feet wide. I tore back the spidery plant's growth and peered down. I could see nothing but an inky darkness. Dropping to my stomach, I turned my head and pointed my ear downward. The last thing I wanted to do was to slip into a crevice of rock that led absolutely nowhere.

I heard the faint sound of scuffling, which told me I was in the right place. Cole had returned to moving packages. I sat up and slipped my gun into the side of my waistband—there wasn't enough space to put it in front or in the small of my back. I would be lucky to get through the narrow opening as it was.

I slipped my feet down through the crevice and set the flat of my hands on either side. I started to lower my body downward while trying to find something for my feet to grab onto so I could leverage my descent. Nothing. All my feet found was empty air.

As I went lower, I rotated my hands and brought my left one across the gap so it was sitting next to my right. I lowered myself down until my arms were fully extended: my chest entering the cave, then my shoulders, and finally my head. I couldn't see anything below. My face was still staring at the wall of rock that formed the cave's ceiling.

I gritted my teeth, hoping that I didn't come down on a sharp piece of jutting rock or that my foot didn't slip on a loose stone, and released my grip. I fell downward into the dark and felt immediate relief as my feet both touched down on a flat surface. I came down into a full squat in an effort to try to absorb any sound created by the impact and remained in that position for several moments as I listened to the faint shuffling still coming from the front of the cave.

I stood up. A bright glow of daylight emanated from the mouth of the cave and I waited patiently for my eyes to adjust to the dimness at my position at the back. Once I could make out the rough outlines and contours of the rocks, I tugged out my weapon and slowly began my advance.

Soon enough I saw Cole's darkened silhouette formed against the daylight. On either side of the cave's walls, large plastic-wrapped bundles of money stood six feet high. I watched as Cole snaked his good arm around a bundle, walked to the other side, and dropped it on top of another. Then he turned and grabbed his gun out from his lower back. He stepped to the side wall and looked out down the length of the ledge.

"You've gone quiet on me, Savage!" When he didn't get any kind of answer, he mumbled something I couldn't make out.

I stepped closer.

"Savage!" he called out, taunting. "Where'd you go, Savage?"

"Right here."

His body jerked in surprise from the unexpected response, and he spun around to face me. My gun's muzzle flickered as I fired a round into his good shoulder. He dropped his gun and cried out in pain. I shot him again, this time in the leg. He collapsed to the floor.

I kicked his gun away and came and stood over him. His face was contorted in agony and every ounce of pride I had witnessed in him earlier was gone. He lay before me in a desperate pile of pain.

"Savage," he said. "I—I'm sorry—"

"Because of you," I interrupted, "a lot of good people are dead." I fired off two more rounds into his chest, just like he'd done to Brad. "I hope it was worth it."

Blood gurgled out from between his lips. He looked up at me with eyes that were quickly losing their vitality. He tried to speak again but couldn't get the words out. His eyes closed and I watched as his chest stopped moving. Then he lay still and the only sounds were the whisper of the wind and the water lapping at the shore below.

I immediately started to look for a radio, frisking Cole's body and looking around the front of the cave. He must have hidden it after realizing that I'd escaped from the buildings. Either that or Vargas had lied to me. I figured either scenario was as likely as the other.

Not wanting to waste any more time, I stepped out of the cave and let my eyes adjust to the sunlight once again as I hurried across the wide ledge and back to the steps. Within a minute I had reached the bottom of the stairs, crossed the sandy beach, and made it into the last remaining boat. I reached for the radio and turned it to channel sixteen. Snatching the microphone, I keyed it and started to speak.

CHAPTER THIRTY-NINE

I RAPPED on the door and announced myself before entering the room. Amy's knuckles were white from her tight grip on the knife. She was kneeling beside Brad. She looked like a frightened fawn. "How is he?" I asked.

She was about to answer when Brad's body shook and he coughed up a spattering of blood. "I don't—I don't feel so great." His face was pallid. "Think you...might be able to get me to a doctor?"

"They're on their way," I said. "Hang in there."

Amy locked eyes with me. "Is it over?"

"Yes. You're safe now."

A wave of relief passed over her face, bringing fresh color with it.

"Hey..." Brad whispered.

I leaned down and brought my ear close. "Yeah?"

"My nurse... Make sure she's hot." Then his head fell back to the floor and he passed out.

Amy gave a stunted grin and shook her head. "Only you, Brad. Only you."

* * *

AMY and I watched as the cable bearing the weight of Brad's unconscious body was reeled in and he was lifted into the air. Inside the chopper, a flight medic reached out the side door, grabbed the rescue basket, and hauled it in. The pilot banked and the rotor wash stirred up a blanket of sea spray as it tore back over the water.

"You think he'll make it?" Amy asked.

"He'll be back with his smart remarks in a couple of days. He's one of the toughest guys I know." We were still waiting on someone to come for us so we turned and headed back to the shade of a few palms. In the meantime I surveyed the rest of the rocky cay, ensuring there was no one else around. In the process I discovered a couple more crevices stuffed with bundles of cash. Finally I heard Amy call out as she pointed east out toward the open water. A two-hundred-seventy-foot Coast Guard MOHAWK cutter was racing toward us, churning water sluicing across its bow.

I couldn't think of anything so welcome.

CHAPTER FORTY

I took the elevator to the fourth floor of Mercy Hospital and turned left down the hall once the doors opened. I knocked on the door to room 408 and went in. The television in the corner was turned to *Jeopardy* and a pink Hello Kitty balloon was tied to the bed railing, floating in the air. Brad was asleep.

I pulled his chart from its holder at the foot of the bed and grabbed a pen. Brad stirred and opened his eyes. "What are you doing?" he asked weakly.

"Looking for the box that says you need an enema. Want to make sure it's checked."

"I'll kill you."

I grinned and replaced the chart, then moved to the side of the bed. Brad's face was missing a lot of its usual color. "How are you feeling?" I asked.

"Like I could win *Jeopardy*."

"I think you already did. You're lucky to be alive."

"Tell me about it." He looked down at his sheets and then back up at me. "Hey, man, thanks for everything you did back there. And for helping to save my life."

"There would have been none of it if you hadn't gotten me out of my bonds. Did they say what your recovery looks like?"

"Probably another couple weeks here and then some physical therapy. Should be back at the job in the next month sometime."

"I'll bring you your laptop so you can file the report on this one."

"That is all you, my friend. Hey, how's Amy doing? I wish I could have shot up those a-holes who treated her that way."

"She's pretty shaken up. Now that we shut everything down, she's going to move in with Roscoe for a while. She doesn't want to go back to the house where Trey was killed." I looked at the balloon and frowned. "What the hell is this?"

"A former commander of mine at Lejeune got wind of my condition. So he sent me that. It's an inside joke."

"Anything I want to know?"

"Nope." He brightened. "Hey, you see my nurse?" A sly glimmer entered his eye. "If they keep her around, I might find a way to stay here even longer."

CHAPTER FORTY-ONE

THERE WAS nothing like enjoying a cold one to celebrate the end of another case, even if Brad wasn't here to join me. Roscoe placed another tall glass of golden liquid before me.

"Tonight," he said, "the bar is yours. Whatever you want, whenever you want, it's on me."

"Thanks, Roscoe."

"You know," he said. "I wish I'd been out there to dice those men up with you." He shook his head in disgust. "I hate that someone would try to hurt Amy like that. Any more information on Trey turn up yet?"

"No, not yet." We all wished that some things had turned out differently. It was going to take Amy a long time to get over Trey's death; there were still a lot of questions as to why he had gotten involved in the first place. We all knew him to be a good kid and still wondered what had compelled him to get into the wrong line of work.

Amy came out of the kitchen and stopped when she saw me. "Hey, Ryan." Her typical, lively demeanor was absent. She was leaving for Orlando tomorrow. Roscoe was giving her a couple weeks' paid leave so she could get away and spend some time with her mother. Everyone hoped the time away might give her a chance to start processing her boyfriend's murder and the trauma of a near rape.

"How are you?" I asked.

She shrugged. "Glad I'm getting away. When I get back, I'm going to find a new place to rent. I don't want to keep living at RC's. He's been great to let me stay with him but I don't want to cramp his style."

"You're his granddaughter, Amy. I seriously doubt you're cramping his style."

She sighed deeply. "I don't know how to do this. Seeing Trey's body like that...losing him..." Her words drifted off.

"It's hard now," I said. "And it will always be hard to some degree. But the pain won't be forever."

Suddenly, Amy's body stiffened. "Oh my God," she said and looked like she'd remembered something. She got a searching look in her eyes and quickly turned around and went back to the bar. Bending down, she disappeared from view for a moment. When she came back up she was clutching her purse.

"You're leaving?" I called after her. But she was distracted and didn't seem to hear. A temporary blaze of light appeared near the front door as she pushed it open and exited the bar.

Roscoe came out of the kitchen a few seconds later, oblivious to what had just happened. "I think your granddaughter just quit," I called out jokingly.

"What?" He looked around the restaurant for her. "What's that mean?"

* * *

AMY GRIPPED the steering wheel tightly as she rode her Nissan down Route 1 like a bat out of hell. Five minutes after tearing out of The Reef's parking lot, she turned into Fitness Forever and went inside. It was a small suite at the end of a strip mall, and the air conditioning was cool against her skin as she approached the front desk. But she paid it no mind. The lady behind the desk was on the phone. She paused her conversation and looked to Amy. "Can I help you?"

Behind the desk was an open floor stuffed with workout equipment—free weights, cable weights, as well as ellipticals and treadmills. Along the back wall was a double-stacked row of lockers.

"Yes," Amy said, "I need to know Trey Johnson's locker number."

The lady frowned. "I'll need to see some ID. Are you on his account?"

Amy fumbled around in her wallet and produced her driver's license. She thought she remembered hearing Trey say that he was going to add her name to his account, but she didn't know if he had or not. She hadn't made it over here to work out since he joined earlier this year. "I think so," she answered.

The lady clicked away on the computer keyboard for a few seconds. "Hmm... Oh, there you are. He's got you on here." Squinting at the screen, she said, "Sixty-four. He's locker number sixty-four."

"Thank you." After the lady handed her license back, Amy made her way to the lockers. She found Trey's on the second stack near the end. A blue combination lock hung on it. She recalled the first group of digits from his phone password and tried that. It worked, and the lock clicked open. She removed it, lifted the lever, and pulled back the door.

Amy thought she might pass out with grief as she picked through his things: a towel, gym shorts and a sleeveless T-shirt, a stick of deodorant, and a pair of earbuds.

A white, unsealed envelope.

She snatched it up and her heart beat faster when she flipped it over and saw what was scratched on the front. *Amy.* Her fingers were trembling now, and she pulled back the envelope flap, plucked out the paper, and unfolded it.

She started to read.

* * *

AFTER AMY LEFT The Reef in the hurried manner she had, I moved over to the bar to talk with Roscoe. Each of us tried to call her several times with no success. So when she walked back in thirty minutes later, we shared a momentary sigh of relief until noticing that her mascara was smeared under her eyes and her nose a bright red. Roscoe hurried out from behind the bar. "Amy, what in the hell? What's going on?"

She shook her head and extended a piece of paper toward her grandfather. Frowning, he unfolded it and read it silently. He muttered under his breath a couple times and then shook his head and let out a deep, long sigh. When he finished, he handed it to me. Surveying it, I saw that it was a note from Trey. I started to read:

Amy,

I hope you never read this. I feel kinda stupid writing it. I know I'm paranoid. Everything will probably blow over soon enough and I'll just throw this out. But in the event that my worries have merit, you need to know something.

A couple months ago, my grandmother's lawyer called me and said that Grandma had recently lost some money to an online scam and that now she hardly had enough money in savings to pay for her residential home up to the end of the year. I didn't tell you because I didn't want to burden you with my problems.

So when a guy I work with—Barry—said I could make some good money working a few nights a week, I went for it. I was just supposed to pick up a package and deliver it. And I never knew what was in it. To be honest, I figured it was something under the table, but I didn't know what else I could do to help Grandma.

I thought it would just be a couple times, that I could make an extra few hundred dollars every month on the side. But over the last week, I've realized that there's no getting out of this, and I'm scared. These are some bad people.

I love you. More than I could ever say or show you. I don't expect you to understand. I'm so sorry that I hurt you.

The letter ended there and wasn't signed. It looked liked Trey hadn't gotten around to finishing it before he was killed. When I looked back up, Roscoe was releasing Amy from a hug. "Where did you find that?" he asked her.

She looked to me. "Ryan, when you said that about forever, I remembered that Trey still had a locker at Fitness Forever. A couple weeks ago, he said something strange. At least, I thought it was at the time. He said that if anything happened to him, I could have whatever was in there. I just told him I wasn't interested in a used deodorant stick. We laughed about it, but something at the time didn't sit right with me." Her eyes started to glisten with tears again. "I completely forgot he said that. Maybe because he was so lighthearted about it."

"I'm really glad he left that for you," I said and then reached in and wrapped my arms around her. "I'm sorry, Amy. He was a great guy. I'll make sure we look into his grandmother's situation and that she's taken care of."

"Yeah," Roscoe said. "We certainly will."

She nodded into my chest, and I held her for a minute while Roscoe stood next to her, looking both angry and sad. I let go of Amy and handed back the letter to her as she wiped at her checks. She sighed and lifted her chin. "Okay," she said resolutely. "Well, I'd better go freshen up in the bathroom."

"You're taking the rest of the day off," Roscoe told her firmly. "Go hang up your apron."

"I'll be okay, RC. The last thing I want to do is sit around thinking about all *this*." She waved the letter in the air. Then she walked off before her grandfather could say any different.

Roscoe shook his head and looked at me. "I love that girl. I hate this for her. It's going to take her a long time to get through it." He patted me on the shoulder and then headed back behind the bar. I returned to my seat on the stool and stared into my beer as I thought.

I found myself wishing that Brad and I had figured out the Barker angle sooner. Had we, Trey might still be alive. That realization stirred up a fresh resolve within me to be a better investigator. It was a stark reminder that in our line of work, people's lives hung in the balance.

A few seats down from me, an older man pulled out his wallet. He withdrew a hundred dollar bill and slid it over to Roscoe to pay for his tab, then waited for his change.

Roscoe held it up to the light and then grabbed his counterfeit detection marker. He tugged off the cap and ran the tip of the marker across the paper. Satisfied, he looked to the customer. "Sorry," he said. "It's not you, but sometimes it's hard for even a trained eye to know a good bill from a bad. There are a lot of bad ones floating out there these days."

I laughed to myself as I finished off my beer. He had no idea just how right he was.

THE END

Ryan's adventures continue in

SAVAGE JUSTICE

After attending a retirement party in Miami for a former Army commander, Ryan Savage wakes to the news of a tragic death in the street just outside his hotel window.

When his gut—honed by fifteen years of chasing down criminals—tells him the death was no accident, he puts his nose to the scent.

Where the trail leads is nothing short of shocking, a secret war being waged on America's most elite warriors, placing Ryan dead center of a conspiracy that reaches into the deepest corners of the U.S. government.

Available now on Amazon

SNEAK PEEK OF SAVAGE JUSTICE

The Middle Eastern night held a chill that had already started to settle into his bones. He really hated the cold. Over the last several years, he had trained in the wet jungles of Brazil, the mountainous forests of Virginia, and the sandy beaches of North Carolina. He didn't mind those. He didn't even mind the deserts—in the daytime. It was the fifty-degree loss of temperature overnight that really got to him.

But tonight wasn't part of any training exercise. This was the real deal.

He focused past the irritant of a low mercury on the ther-mometer and continued to pan the horizon with his night vision binoculars, alternating his gaze between the open desert to his left and the barren ridge above the cliffs to his left.

The young E-5 Delta Force operator was on overwatch on top of a neutral ridge. His pack lay on the ground in front of him. On it rested the barrel of his Heckler and Koch

416 carbine—designated the M27. The assault rifle was chambered in 5.56 NATO and had a 16.5-inch barrel. With a multi-position telescopic buttstock and proprietary gas piston system, the weapon was incredibly accurate. There was no other frontline battle rifle that compared.

Above the soldier, a hundred thousand stars twinkled against the black mantel of the desert sky. Two hundred meters downslope his troop lay asleep, tucked into their RON ("remain overnight") hide along the base of a rising cliff face.

He had already gotten his sleep for the night. But he still felt unusually tired. When his turn in the rotation came up, it had taken his Sergeant Major two full minutes to wake him. After plenty of prodding, shaking, and cursing it finally took the toe of the ranking soldier's boot in his ribs to wake him from his slumber.

That was almost two hours ago. But even now he couldn't seem to shake the weariness he felt in his eyes and the muddled haziness he was experiencing between his ears. It was like he had taken a sleeping pill and couldn't shake it off. They had just under an hour before BMNT ("Beginning of morning nautical twilight")—dawn—when they would pack up and continue on to their final waypoint. Maybe the movement would serve to wake him up.

He saw a shudder of movement in the distance and zoomed in near where his troop was sleeping. His commander, Major Dennis Archer, was out of his bag. He lay a hand against the face of the cliff and leaned over as though looking at his feet. His mouth suddenly yawed open and the E-5 watched his Major vomit up the contents of his stomach. He wiped his mouth on the back of his sleeve and then stumbled along the base of the cliff like a town drunk, his knees buckling, his head moving from side to side. He walked twenty yards into the open and started shaking his head like he was trying to rid his ears of an irritating song.

What he did next sent an eerie chill down the back of his E-5 on overwatch.

Major Archer kneeled down on the desert floor beside a rock the size of a small chair. He placed his hands on either side and, with no thought to pain or consequences began to bash his forehead on the top of the rock. *Thunk.* He did it again. *Thunk.* Again. *Thunk.*

His E-5 flinched and keyed the mic of his multiband inter/intra team radio. "Commander. *Commander*. What are you doing?"

Thunk.

His commander was not responding.

Thunk.

"Team 8, this is Crawler. *Wake the hell up!*"

Thunk.

His team was not responding. Everyone was mic'd. Out here you didn't sleep without your earpiece in. No one, however, was stirring.

Blood was pouring down the officer's face. His movements were slower now, and he started to wobble from side to side.

Another flutter of movement came from the troop's hide. The operator on overwatch turned his attention to it and watched as his Sergeant Major and the troop's ranking

NCO, Hopper Carlson, stumbled away from the three remaining operators still asleep on the ground. As if viewing a rerun the E-5 watched as his Sergeant Major struggled away from on legs that looked like they were about to give out. He leaned over, set his hands on his knees, and evacuated the contents of his stomach. He wretched for half a minute until there was nothing left to come up. Then he removed his hands from his knees and stood.

A gunshot rattled across the dark stillness of the desert.

The Major's body was sprawled across the rock, the side of his head now displaying a massive hole where the bullet had found its exit.

The E-5 had a fleeting thought that perhaps this was some kind of hazing. the first mission as a special force warrior, as a full-blown Delta Operator.

But the hopeful idea quickly faded as he recalled the nature of their mission and the prevalence of known insurgents within the general region. This was not a hazing, it was not a soldier's version of a collegiate prank. Whatever was happening out there was real. It was nightmarish and real, the scene from a hideous and distasteful horror movie.

He returned his attention to his Sergeant Major, who had moved five yards from his previous position. He was staring down toward his feet now, unmoving. leaned down and picked up a large rock in both hands. Then he started hitting himself in the face with it.

"Sergeant Major!" What in God's name was happening? "Sergeant Major Carlson!"

Thunk.

Suddenly, Carlson dropped the rock and let out a blood-curdling scream. He grabbed both his ears and shook his head before kicking at the dirt while running in a tight circle.

"Sergeant Major!"

Carlson stopped abruptly. He looked up at the stars and blinked. And before his subordinates knew what was happening he withdrew his sidearm, set it to his temple, and pressed the trigger. His head kicked to one side and his body crumbled to the ground.

The E-5's hands were trembling now. He had been trained for nearly every possible scenario on the battlefield. But he had been fully unprepared to watch his two superiors suddenly act as if they were possessed and then take their own lives. While on a mission no less. Everyone had seemed fine before they settled in for the night: jokes, quiet laughter, and easy banter.

He keyed the microphone to his satellite radio. "Eagle Base, this is Crawler 03. Come in."

He waited several seconds. "Eagle Base reads Crawler 03. Go ahead."

"Eagle we have—have a problem. Streak and Rover are down."

There was a pause. "Say again Crawler 03. Did you make enemy contact?"

"*Negative*. Streak and Rover *are dead*. They came out of their bags and—and killed themselves with their own pistols. One—one right after the other."

He knew he was speaking with Corporal Robins. The base Lieutenant Colonel would still be asleep, if not just waking.

"Standby Crawler 03."

He waited for what felt like an eternity. He used the uneasy silence to surveyed the carnage below, still unable to believe what his eyes had seen. He looked back to the hide. Still, no one stirred. These were the kind of warriors who would wake if a feather touched down within thirty years of their position. But now two gunshots had gone off in close proximity and yet they continued to sleep.

Finally, a deep voice pierced the silence–the voice of Colonel Art Dunford. "Crawler 03, this is Solo 1. Please repeat."

He recited his previous transmission, telling the officer of the odd and unsettling behavior of his Major and then his Sergeant Major before they took their own lives without a moment's hesitation.

"What is your position?"

"I'm on overwatch. Franks, Colton, and Smith are in their bags in the position relayed to base last night. I can't get them to wake. They're not responding to me."

Another long pause. "And no enemy contact? Before or after the... events."

"No, sir."

"A bird is in the air. Twenty-two minutes out. Stay on overwatch for ten and then make your way down and join your troop. Try and rouse them if you can."

"Yes, sir."

"Eagle, out."

He set the mic down and stared off into the distance. This wasn't real. It couldn't be real.

A wave of exhaustion washed over him again, causing a mild panic to well up inside. *What the hell was going on?* He suddenly remembered his gas mask, buried inside his pack. He scrambled to his knees and slid his rifle to the side. Lifting up his pack he tore through it and located the mask. He pulled it out, removed his helmet, and slipped the mask over his face, then pulled the straps taught.

There were no WMDs in Afghanistan, and he had no explanation for what was going on. But maybe local insurgents had released a toxin or nerve gas the air.

He kept his eyes downslope and scanned the horizon, trying to avoid looking at the bodies of his dead leaders as he listened to his shaky breaths echoing inside his mask.

He was no longer thinking about how cold he was.

* * *

Ryan's adventures continue in Savage Justice:

Get It Now on Amazon…

STAY UP TO SPEED...

To be notified of upcoming releases as soon as they come out, sign up at http://bit.ly/2pESrFX.

Follow Jack on Facebook: fb.me/jackhardinauthor

Say hello: jack.w.hardin00@gmail.com

ABOUT THE AUTHOR

Jack Hardin currently lives in Arlington, TX, with his stunning wife and five kiddos, the latter who all range from 3-16 years.

He grew up in an Army family and spent half his childhood living in Germany, traveling all over Europe prior to the fall of the Iron Curtain. At nine years old he walked through Checkpoint Charlie and into East Berlin just one year before the Berlin Wall came down. He holds a 2nd degree black belt in Taekwondo, is proficient with bo staff and nunchucks, and has taught women's self-defense.

Those alone do not make him awesome, but it all sounds really cool.

You can be the first to be notified of Jack's newest pre-orders by liking his Facebook page. And sometimes he'll posts other cool stuff there, too.